THE KNIGHT OF ROMANCE

A NOVEL-IN-STORIES

Lane Roberts

Quill·Hound
PUBLISHING, LLC

QUILL HOUND PUBLISHING, LLC TRADE PAPERBACK EDITION, JULY 2025

Published in the United States by Quill Hound Publishing, LLC.

This is a work of fiction. Names, characters, places, and incidents either are the product of the author's imagination or used fictitiously. Any resemblance to actual persons, living or dead, events, or locales is entirely coincidental.

The Cataloging-in-Publication Data is on file at the Library of Congress.

Quill Hound Publishing, LLC Trade Paperback ISBN: 978-1-967851-00-3

Ebook ISBN: 978-1-967851-01-0

www.quilldhoundpublishing.com

Printed in the United States of America.

A Whisper Of Gratitude

A special thank you to "Ted's Mom", whose gentle nudge dared me to wade into these waters, and to "Crush", who taught me how to swim.

The Man Behind The Glass

Ahhhh, my dear reader.

There is no need to linger in this drafty hallway, please, come in. I have a warm fire for you and a rich selection of private wing back chairs, cozy chaise lounges, and cushy leather sofas for you to snuggle into. Welcome to my private library. Oh, I should probably introduce myself. I am Morgan Knight, curator of romantic tales. Like a rare art collector, I scour the world looking for those stories that linger within us, long after the final page has been turned. And my library? Well, that's for you to enjoy. Here you will find the echoes of stolen glances, shadows of temptations and caverns of veiled passions.

My search has taken me from finding couples walking on sandy, Italian beaches at midnight to overhearing them enjoying their breakfasts together on luxurious country patios. I have witnessed the miracles of these romantic tales and how they can awaken forgotten desires, mend broken dreams, and seduce us into believing in love all over again. I am, if you would indulge the title, "The Knight Of Romance".

You have wandered in here because the ordinary no longer satisfies. But, before you turn the page, I should echo a word of caution. These stories are not for the timid. Like romance itself, they smolder, unraveling something deep within us that is far more intoxicating. Perhaps, even wickedly erotic. Within these pages, desire breathes through the words. The imagery those words create are designed to tempt, unsettle, and awaken. If you dare to surrender to them, they may reveal parts of you long forgotten or parts that you never expected to find.

I have cracked the spines of these leather-bound volumes that line my bookshelves to unleash their sensual history. And now, they are here for you to discover, as I set aside a special selection just for you. Like a curated flight of wine, I have selected nine stories designed to intoxicate your imagination, awaken your senses, and set your pulse racing.

Each tale is accompanied at the beginning with a quick personal note. Consider that note an intimate whisper describing the story's romantic essence as one might savor the bouquet of a rare vintage. To heighten that pleasure, my note includes a suggested pairing for a carefully selected wine, cocktail, coffee, or zero proof elixir which mirrors the unique flavor of the story.

My private library is a sanctuary of shadows and longing, curated for your indulgence. Here, every tale waits behind a door that opens only to the softest knock, preserving the hush-hush nature of the story, and ensuring your solitude.

And, if you long for a deeper connection, I invite you to join me beyond these pages at www.*TheKnightOfRomance*.com, where I can alert you to secret letters and private musings that might intrigue you. I assure you with all the trust that I can muster that there's never any cluttering correspondence. Rather, just a simple means for us to keep in touch with one another.

But for now, let us raise a glass to romance, whether it be the innocent first kiss or the raw passion of a forbidden affair. I promise you, there is a story here meant just for you. Allow yourself to be entranced by the scent of the aged leather and the rich mahogany. Pour yourself a glass. Let the words unfold around you. Allow the desire in these pages to find you. The fire is warm. And here, in my library, romance is always in the air.

Gallantly yours,

Morgan Knight, The Knight of Romance

Your Flight Of Stories

Some love stories are carefully written, others are whispered in stolen moments. Teresa's was neither. Hers was a fleeting collision, a lingering "what if" that haunted her for years. Fifteen years ago, a single kiss - daring, reckless, and wordless - shared with a stranger had branded itself onto Teresa's memory. That single event served as a crutch she could rely upon through every heartbreak and the turbulent trials of life. He was a fantasy that she clung to, a secret indulgence that also surfaced during her private, quiet moments. He became the kind of daydream that made the world feel a little less heavy. However, our daydreams and fantasies are not meant to cross into reality. But for Teresa, reality had other plans.

On the highway of life, Erin was usually a cautious driver, applying the brakes to any suggestion of vulnerability and keeping her desires hidden under the hood. Until now. Every time she stepped into Enzo's coffee shop, her pulse quickened. The aroma of freshly ground beans mixed with the thrill of seeing him behind the counter driving new and intoxicating thrills through her. He was an alluring mystery, a man who once lived life on the edge, as a Formula One driver, but now steered toward quieter moments, or so Erin thought. As she sipped her macchiato, her thoughts drifted into the imagination lane, wondering what it would be like to be caught in his gaze as he shifted through her gears. Buckle up. This ride isn't what it seems.

Michele always saw herself as a powerful, independent woman - bold enough to spell her name with a single "L" and unapologetic about possessing the sex drive of a man. She was not the sort of woman who got stood up - until tonight.

There's no denying the sting to the ego when this happens. The real question is, will she let it leave a mark, or will she rise up and prove her personal power? With the help of an effortlessly, handsome stranger, a darkened movie theater becomes the setting for something silent, private, and electric. As she did with her own name, Michele just might be able to rewrite heartache into heat, turning a disappointing evening into something wickedly unforgettable.

Horsin' Around 59

Kayla knew how to play the part. In her town of majestic horse farms and grain towers, she was the picture of grace. Loyal. Hard working. The "good girl" that the town expected her to be. Their reflections brought her peace - but not freedom. What would they say, if they knew her secret? Then, a wild horse rode back into her life. The town's folk whispered their warnings and savage stories. He was untamed. Unapologetic. Someone to be avoided. But so was she. They just didn't know it. Finally, there's a chance for Kayla - because oftentimes, the most dangerous path is the only one that leads to freedom.

Beneath The Surface 82

Noelle returned to her lakefront hometown, bracing for a flood of memories. Instead, she got drenched by the splash of newness. Gone were the reminders of long-lost summers with their scent of pines and tranquil sounds of waves lapping beneath the dock. Now, there were new homes. New docks. And, new people. But the lakes were not the only thing that had changed. The boy next door, a connection rooted in childhood, had grown to be the kind of man who steals glances. As a boy, he had chased her with shy admiration. That longing was quiet and deep. Noelle could not help to wonder if the tide he once held for her still pulled him beneath the surface, and if maybe those waters were waiting to rise again.

Memphis Momentum.................................... 100

Vanna stepped onto the Memphis trolley never imagining that a pair of broken sunglasses would fan a whirlwind encounter with a Southern gentleman. Still healing from her divorce, she never thought that she would have to imagine life with someone new. The first glance. The first kiss. The first time. But her ex's disrespect forced her to reimagine such things. Letting him go was easy, letting go of her commitment - another matter. Her Asian heritage was steeped in honor, a concept that also echoes through American Southern tradition. But, a patient and playful gentleman may just have the strength to help her unravel the past, and her guarded resistance.

His Place, Her Rules 120

An eternity had passed since Brooke shuffled with the steps of dating. She felt out of her element. Time had weathered her, chipping away pieces until she scarcely recognized her own reflection. She once moved through life with a bold rhythm. Now, she let the music carry her, more spectator than star. But tonight, opportunity set her dance card ablaze, filling out the remaining spots with chance and daringness. Tonight, both her smile and her eyes held secrets again, and her gaze spoke a language that only the bold understood. Brooke's true journey was beginning tonight, not towards romance. But, towards herself. Towards the forgotten fire that once burned through her, and the thrilling possibility that those flames were never truly gone.

Shifting Gears 135

Abigail never intended for the night to take such a turn. Her love-less marriage, and her husband's stubborn pride had left her with an impossible choice, one dictated more by biology. Mother Nature had a plan for her, though. Realizing that Abigail was stuck in a late-night garage with a young mechanic, she knew his hands could fix far more than just busted brake lines. She spoke to Abigail. Her message - primal. Now, as Abigail watches him work, that reckless thought, embedded by Mother Nature, takes root and sends a thrill through Abigail that has nothing to do with super cars. Regardless of the choices laying before her, Abigail learns one thing is certain. In the end, Mother Nature always wins.

A personal favorite of mine, this tale weaves through the familiar threads of romance, adventure and forbidden love. Yet, within the story's embrace lies a unique twist, and one that I have yet to encounter in romantic storytelling. This journey unfolds solely through the first person eyes of a young man.

What is it like to plunge into love as a young man while also wrestling with the growing pains of manhood? Do men believe in fate, or connections that defy reason? What does a man think about during romantic moments? Tapping into raw and untamed energy, the story explores these questions, offering an unapologetically masculine lens on love and desire. This is an erotic odyssey that, I am told, leaves women weak in the knees. Rich with raw cravings and masculine introspection, this narrative unfurls a journey so potent that it leaves hearts captivated.

The Guy

Bold and deeply layered, this story opens with notes of nostalgia and unspoken longing, revealing a bouquet of bittersweet memory, temptation, and fate. The initial taste is smooth, ripe with warmth and youthful recklessness, reminiscent of a rain-soaked kiss under summer skies. But as the story lingers, hints of matured desire and unfulfilled dreams rise to the surface, creating a rich complexity.

Suggested Pairings

Wine: Château Cheval Blanc 2015

Cocktail: The Boulevardier

Coffee: Vanilla Rose Latte

Zero Proof: Black Cherry and Rosemary Sparkler

Unwind
Morgan Knight

I've shared the secrets behind these drinks at www.*TheKnightOfRomance*.com, should you care to indulge.

"I never..." Teresa's girlfriend hesitated, holding her wine glass high, as if she were delivering a toast. In actuality, she was daring herself to finish the sultry thought. Her eyes flicked nervously to the jesting grins of the girls gathered around her. Finally, with a deep breath, the courage surfaced. "I never... went down on a guy... in a public place."

The room erupted into nervous laughter, jeers, and a chorus of "Oh my God!" from the tribe of girlfriends surrounding their sleep over circle. Comfy pajamas. Pillows. And wine, of course wine. Glasses were raised in unison, though only one woman took a sip. Her bold admission quickly met with flying pillows, friendly jibes, and playful cries of, "You sluuuuttt!"

Girls' weekend. Not just any girls' weekend, though. Teresa had known these women since college. These were deep rooted friendships. Solid. Tested over years, into marriages, through divorces, around children, - up, down, over and under all of the unpredictable twists and perils of life. Together, they stepped forward into adulthood and now they navigated life's hazards with an unshakable bond. Reliable. Like I said, tested.

Every summer, they returned to their alma mater, Notre Dame. No, not the cathedral in Paris. South Bend, Indiana. One member would rent a house for the weekend, and the others would pitch in with plane tickets, Uber rides, and naturally - wine. Always wine.

The circle was buzzing when one of the women turned to Teresa, her grin mischievous. "Teresa's got a story like that."

"No, I don't," Teresa shot back quickly.

"Oh, come on," the woman teased, dragging out her words. "You know. The guuuuuuyyyy?!?"

Teresa raised her brow. "What guy?", her tone deceptive and lightly defensive.

Another chimed in, her eyes alight with recognition. "Oh yeah! I remember. Go on. Tell them about 'The Guy,' Teresa."

Teresa hesitated. She had known exactly who they meant the moment the topic surfaced. The story of "The Guy" wasn't just a college fling. The tale had taken on a kind of mythic quality over the years for Teresa. The story resembled a drama but was more a historical tale stretching back to those college years. She had stopped at an enclosed ATM vestibule, when "The Guy" strolled in, holding the trifecta hand for attraction: tall, dark, and handsome. But he also held a bonus pair of pocket kings: athleticism and charm. That's a tough hand to beat. Young and inexperienced, Teresa found herself utterly captivated by his presence, as though she'd been transported to another world just by standing near him.

The vestibule housed two ATMs, each with its own small line. Teresa and "The Guy" ended up at opposing machines, a silent exchange unfolding between them as they waited in line. Without saying a word, they began a playful, unspoken conversation through fleeting glances and coy gestures. Teresa brushed a strand of hair from her face while his Irish green eyes danced from the floor... over to Teresa...then cast onto the ceiling, but they always returned back to her.

His shyness eventually dissolved, and when she caught a true look of those eyes, they weren't just green; they shifted, deepening to a mossy hue when shadows touched them. In the right light, they held the power to disarm her, as though staring into a forest at dawn - calm, endless, and dangerous. His gaze lingered, intense and knowing, as if he could see every thought that she was too afraid to speak. And when he looked at her, really looked, she felt like drowning in something wild and untamed, something she didn't want to escape.

She debated whether to say something, maybe ask him a casual question, but youth has a way of wrapping us in self-doubt. Her inexperience and self-consciousness held her firmly in place. Slowly, the lines moved forward until they were both standing at their respective ATMs, the last two in the vestibule. Teresa's nerves bubbled up. She rushed through the screen prompts, suddenly hyper aware of her actions. She knew she looked flustered but couldn't figure out why. The machine's gears whirled as if taking an eternity to dispense her cash, feeding her growing impatience.

Finally - BEEP. The screen flashed the prompt to collect her cash, card, and receipt. Teresa snagged her card, stuffing it into her clutch along with her cash, then zipping the small bag within a wink. She ripped the receipt from the machine while pivoting toward the door when - BAM! She collided directly into him, just as he turned from his own machine.

He was taller, much taller. Her head had bumped squarely into his chest. The impact slowed her chaotic urgency, almost as if hitting pause on the moment. Her social recovery plan was simple: look up and apologize. But...those eyes...those late Spring green eyes...their mesmerizing effect. When her's met his', everything around them faded. His nearness sent a ripple through her, like a storm brewing just beneath Teresa's skin. Her thoughts became a blur of sensations. Childish words floated to her mind: "princess," "forever," and "Disney." She couldn't explain why, but she felt swept up in something larger than herself, which made her nearly drop her clutch while her ATM receipt slipped away, floating like a feather between his feet.

On instinct, Teresa rose onto her toes, her hand trailing upward to the back of his head. Gently, she pulled him closer and kissed him. For a moment, he froze, caught off guard. But then, slowly, his lips softened, and the kiss deepened into something meaningful. They hadn't exchanged a single word, yet the connection between them felt almost otherworldly, as if this existed on a plane beyond reason.

And then, just as suddenly as the whole thing had started, Teresa bolted.

"WHAT?" The collective gasp from her girlfriends was deafening, their disbelief palpable. Questions came rapid-fire. "How could you?" "Why?" "Where is he now?" "I don't get it!"

Teresa shook her head, her whispered reply unwavering. "I don't know. I don't know."

The group eventually dispersed, frustrated by the lack of a satisfying ending to her story. But for Teresa, the memory of the mysterious young man lingered. This wasn't the first time. Over the years, she had replayed that encounter countless times, imagining alternate endings and weaving "what if" scenarios into the fabric of her regrets. Whenever she endured heartbreak, another failed relationship or a rough breakup, her mind inevitably drifted back to him.

He had become her emotional anchor, the centerpiece of every fantasy she used to soothe herself. Even her private, "me times" or personal fantasy experience came back to their shared emotional center. The memory of that fleeting, unexplained connection brought her comfort, with underlying longing. That night, as always, thoughts of him lulled her to sleep, leaving her with romantic and erotic dreams of what might have been.

~ ~

The next morning greeted the women with an air of excitement, as though the day held an adventure waiting to unfold. The group had splintered into smaller clusters, exploring a lively street fair. Teresa found herself gravitating toward two of her former roommates, the ones she felt most at ease with, the ones who allowed her to be her true self. The others? Still cherished friends, but some friendships demanded the expectation of "good girl" perfection, a performance Teresa needed to momentarily step away from. For now, she was happily assigned to "1st Battalion, Fun Company," where laughter and lightheartedness replaced judgment.

As they wandered past cotton candy vendors, carnival game booths, and stalls of amateur artists, Teresa's squad leader convinced her to sit for a portrait by a bohemian-artist. The attractive, middle-aged woman had surrounded her makeshift studio with energy globes and aura beads which created a soothing sensation. Teresa accepted the order without any resistance to the idea. With a playful shrug, she perched herself on the artist's creaky wooden chair like a bird settling into its nest.

From her seat, Teresa kept an eye on her two roommates, who stood behind the artist, watching the drawing take shape. At first, their faces were lit with curiosity, but soon their expressions began to shift. Puzzlement crept in. The two exchanged glances, their brows furrowing slightly.

"What?" Teresa asked, smirking.

Neither answered. One leaned closer to get a better look while the other squinted, her head tilting slightly. Teresa's curiosity turned into uneasiness. "What's she drawing? Is it a caricature?" she asked, laughing nervously.

Still, no answer. Finally, one of her friends took a step towards the artist, as if ready to intervene, but the other grabbed her arm and pointed to a small sign next to the artist. They both stared at the sign for a moment, then exchanged knowing nods. The first retreated back to her spot, her expression now returning to her original curiosity.

Teresa raised an eyebrow. "What did you guys get me into?" she teased, settling back into the chair.

For a brief moment, silence reigned between them. The ambient buzz of the fair blended into a distant, muffled hum. The only distinct sound was the scratch of the artist's charcoal pencil, a rhythmic, almost hypnotic noise against the canvas. Teresa drifted into a gentle, meditative trance, as if this bohemian woman were pulling fragments of joy from her, like whispers of light, and weaving them into the canvas.

Before Teresa could stir herself from her peaceful daydreaming, the bohemian woman peeked from behind the canvas, a soft "All done" escaping her lips. She stepped aside, revealing her creation. Teresa rose slowly, her gaze catching the playful glint in her friends' eyes as she rounded the easel. The artist turned the canvas toward her, and time seemed to shatter into stillness.

Her breath caught, as she folded both hands around her lips. Her chest tightened. Color drained from her face, leaving her ashen, as if she'd come face to face with a ghost.

Her friends erupted into laughter, one of them throwing an arm around her shoulders. "He's handsome, isn't he?" they teased.

But Teresa could not respond. She could not move. Her wide eyes were fixed on the portrait, her mind swirling. Finally, she managed to whisper one word: "How?"

One of her friends giggled. "How what?" She pointed to the artist's posting.

The sign read: *I will draw your soulmate.*

What her friends did not know was that the gypsy artist had captured *him*. The boy from the ATM, some fifteen years ago. The gypsy artist had somehow drawn...*The Guy.*

~ ~

Teresa held the portrait in both hands, her fingers tracing its edges as though the image might slip away. Another platoon of girlfriends wandered into the portrait tent, buzzing with their usual banter. One chatted about a guy selling handmade earrings, another was on the hunt for deep fried Snickers bars. But Teresa did not hear them. She remained transfixed, her thoughts locked on the drawing.

One of the ladies from the invading friendship squad, chomping gum and cradling an almost empty fountain drink, sidled up to Teresa. She shook her cup, the crushed ice rattling like an impatient complaint. "Where's Aiden?" she asked, her words casual yet cutting through the chatter.

Teresa's squad exchanged puzzled looks. "Who's Aiden?" one of them asked.

The gum chomper took one last, loud sip of air from her straw before gesturing at Teresa's portrait with the drink as her pointer. "Aiden. Where's Aiden?"

A hush fell over the group. Even the gum chewing paused, the woman now twirling her gum between her teeth as she sensed the weight of the moment. A friend from Teresa's group stepped forward, her tone guarded. "That's not...Aiden. That's *The Guy*. Teresa's guy. Who's Aiden?"

But the gum chomper scoffed, her tone a blend of mockery and certainty. "No... *That's* Aiden. We went to school with him. He's the soccer coach now."

Teresa's breath twitched. "What?"

"He coaches soccer," the girl said, her voice matter-of-fact.

Another friend jumped in. "Wait, where?"

"Here," Gum Chomper replied, as if this were the most obvious thing in the world. Her voice dipped into sarcasm. "What do you mean, *where?*"

Teresa's squad leader pressed further, pointing at the portrait. "So, you're telling me the guy in this picture is the Notre Dame soccer coach?"

"Uh-huh." The gum popped loudly, sealing her reply.

"And he's the guy Teresa told us about last night?"

Gum chomper shrugged and gestured lazily at Teresa. "I guess so. Ask her."

All eyes turned to Teresa, whose fingers traced the jawline of the portrait. Her voice was barely audible. "That's him."

Excitement ignited the group like a spark hitting dry kindling. One friend blurted, "This only happens in movies!" Another repeatedly muttered, "Holy shit. Holy shit." Someone finally voiced what they were all thinking: "We've gotta find him."

Teresa remained frozen, not responding to any of their excitement. The noise surrounding her faded as tension brewed, dripping into her mug of anxiety. For years, *The Guy* had been her escape, a pillar. She leaned on him through fantasy whenever life dealt from the bottom of the deck or fucked up the shuffle. But now, with reality closing in, she couldn't help but wonder, would the real him measure up to the dream? Would that emotional crutch be there if she ever needed it?

When she finally emerged from her trance, the second platoon of girls had nearly vanished. She watched them fade into the crowd, stumbling over one another with determined energy. Alarmed, she asked, "Where are they going?"

A comrade from her own unit hesitated before replying, "I think... they're going...to get him."

Teresa's shoulders slumped. What had been a deeply personal moment for her was quickly turning into a schoolyard spectacle. Recognizing her distress, one former roommate said, "We should get her home."

"Before they get back," the other agreed.

~ ~

At the rented house, Teresa sat on the edge of her bed, staring at the portrait resting on her lap. "How could the artist have known?" she murmured. The gypsy who sketched the drawing had captured something that felt almost supernatural. At times, Teresa leaned into ideas of a "forever person". A Hallmark Christmas movie might nudge her into embracing "happily ever after", but the effect never lingered for more than an hour or two. Real life eventually picked up where fantasy left off for Teresa. "Reality comes crashing down" had always been her default sentiment.

She was still lost in thought when Elina entered the room. Though not a close friend, Elina's serene presence had always been a quiet source of comfort. Elina hadn't attended the university, and to Teresa, she was more of an acquaintance. She had been a peripheral "friend of a friend" who had permeated the group over the years and eventually evolved into another loving member.

A bit eccentric. Well-traveled. Well spoken. Accepting of all. Elina's kindness was rare. Genuine. Almost palpable. She loved nature. And on first glance, most people would think that she would have loved the 60's, but we're all born into time period's we don't belong in.

"Oh. I didn't know that you were in here, Teresa. I am so sorry to disturb you," Elina whispered. "I just need something from my bag."

In truth, Teresa appreciated the kindness of the interruption. Again, Elina offered comforting company everywhere she went. Teresa felt like she was hanging out with someone who possessed the combined wisdom of a parent, a grandparent, and three generations of great grandparents. But that wisdom was never flaunted. No one would ever know this by looking at her.

Teresa smiled faintly. "You're fine. I'm embarrassed for being such a drama queen."

"Shush," Elina said softly. "Childhood memories can get overwhelming at times."

Teresa waited to respond. She was remembering. While Elina waited to listen. She was supporting.

"I was nineteen," Teresa laughed in a weak tone.

"Still developing," Elina replied with quiet certainty. Her argument was two words, yet simple, direct, accepting, and undeniably solid. Teresa felt an instant connection. She appreciated feeling seen.

Teresa pressed for more wisdom, "Can I ask you something?"

Elina smiled, "About your crush?"

Teresa hesitated, stumbling over her words and her fear of seeming foolish. Her thoughts pervaded. Those thoughts were stuck in the mud. Elina sat patiently on the opposing bed, while Teresa pried the thoughts free from her mental tar pit. Clearly Elina had already endeared herself to Teresa, even close friends had trouble extending such charitable depths, but Elina's graceful essence bordered on an artform.

Her thoughts were liberated in chunks as Teresa stumbled through them, "I don't know him. He's just a fantasy.

"A fantasy that you kissed," Elina's words brought Aiden into reality a bit more. She had indeed touched him, in real life. She had a moment with him, in real life.

Teresa chuckled. "Yeah, but I was just a girl."

Elina's tone softened further as she drove straight to the heart of the matter "What is your biggest fear with this situation?"

Teresa trusted the candor of the question. She didn't even have to think before replying. She knew. "That if I meet him again, I'll lose the *idea* of him, the thing I lean on when life gets hard. Which inevitably happens."

Elina consumed the thought with a head nod. Teresa watched as Elina's mind chewed on her reply. She shot back with another equally gentle question, "All those times you leaned on the idea of him, do you think those moments would have been much easier if he were *actually* there to lean on?"

Teresa blinked, struck by the logic. She had no option but to capitulate with another smile.

Elina continued, her replies somehow now even more sympathetic, "There's always risk with the heart," Elina continued. "But with smart decisions, the rewards outweigh risks."

As Elina's simple logic burned through excuse after excuse, Teresa warmed herself with their incineration. Teresa could feel herself being set free. She shared a coyish smile when Elina accurately teased her about the inevitable number of dirty thoughts Teresa had likely had regarding Aiden over the years.

Her closing arguments were simply far too convincing to deny, "Here's the thing, Teresa. All those times that you leaned on the idea of Aiden.

That's not what got you through those times. *YOU* got you through those times. *HE* was simply an idea. The real strength was already within you. The only choice now is, will you decide to turn *'the idea of him'* into *'the reality of him...and maybe enjoy life a little more from his presence'?"*

Teresa heard the faint echoes of clanking metal. Her emotional chains were loosening, and as the full effect of Elina's wisdom struck her, Teresa heard the thud of those chains crashing to the floor.

Elina stood and moved to Teresa. She wrapped her arms around Teresa, offering an embrace so genuine it felt like a weighted blanket of love that had been warmed by the glow of a comforting fire. Friends like this were truly rare.

And just as smoothly as Elina had glided into the room, her presence evaporated.

~ ~

Moments later, Teresa emerged from the bedroom. Second Platoon, Giggle Company had returned from their scouting mission, accounting details regarding Aiden. Their seventh grade-like exuberance still percolated as one squad member squealed, "He's going to meet you."

Another assisted in the sentence, "Tonight. At 7:00"

The third squad member finished the report, "After practice. At the soccer complex".

As if on cue, the three voices came together in a trio saying, "He's taking you out".

Teresa chuckled at their ridiculous performance. Two girls fell into the background, taking their shared dialogue about how hot Aiden looked with them. The third approached Teresa. She stated that Aiden said he was not normally into blind dates but considering that a gaggle of girls were campaigning for him, he considered the occasion.

Bathing in her newfound freedom, Teresa relished in her excitement. Her respiration and heart rate were accelerating, and Aiden wasn't even in the room.

She recalled again how during her "me times", if the novel that she was reading or the movie that she was watching wasn't doing the job for her, Aiden's memory always pushed her over the edge. In those fantasies she and Aiden had done everything: making love, quickies at work, hand jobs, blow jobs. Oh, and she'd lost count of the number of times he'd gone down on her. That was always the score kicker for her. Those fantasies extended into places, as well: bathtubs, kitchen countertops, backseats, closets at weddings, luxurious hotel rooms, even the 50-yard line of Notre Dame Stadium. The priests would have had a field day with that one.

Teresa chuckled to herself that she'd probably had more fantasy sex with Aiden than she'd ever had actual sex with any boyfriend. If there was any remaining grip of anxiety for Teresa, these fantasies were the source. She forgave herself, because such anxiety made natural sense. Years of their slow-burning buildup flashed through her mind, igniting a thrill she could not contain. This was no longer just a story she told herself. This was becoming real.

~ ~

As 7:00 approached, Teresa slipped out quietly, feeling more like she was orchestrating a prison break than heading out for a date. She wanted to avoid the inquisition from her girlfriends, knowing she'd face their "press conference" later. For now, she reveled in the bravery of venturing into uncharted emotional territory.

Indiana summer nights are warm and sticky. Every year, some local utters the same tiresome old maxim, "It's not the heat, it's the humidity." Evenings do offer a little relief, but it's never "good sleeping weather", another Midwest adage. Teresa accounted for the sticky evening by selecting a light sundress and Jessica Simpson sandals. She had always doubted her selection in footwear, and though the sandals had a heel, she knew the leggy

Texan understood sexy shoes better than she. She had no problem following Simpson's lead.

The rhythmic click of those heels echoed along the bike path leading to the soccer complex. She expected nostalgia to wash over her, but her emotional tank was already topped off with Aiden anticipation. In the distance, she could see the soccer field lights reflecting off the surrounding treetops. Those lights were a homing beacon, pulling each of her steps closer to reality.

When she cleared the trees, she could distinguish the entire field. In the distance, several young men chanted around a central figure. Their husky young voices chanted in unison, "Notre Dame, Our Mother!" They clapped together in perfect rhythm and peeled away from the central figure. They swiftly gathered like a flock at the bleachers before scattering - some grabbing their bikes, others jogging back to their dorms. That central figure that was left behind? Aiden, sitting alone in the bleachers, tapping notes into his iPad. Practice was over.

Teresa followed the curve of the path around the field and approached the metal stands. Aiden sat five rows up. Teresa's nervousness? Surprisingly, none. She had just a simple nugget of pride, reflected by the courage it was taking for her to face whatever it was that she was facing. Aiden looked up at her, after hearing her heels approaching the bleachers.

"Are you my blind date?" he teased with a polite smirk.

"You could say that," Teresa replied, smiling. She realized that before their date began that she should probably at least allude to how they know one another, that their interaction had not been entirely by chance. She understood that perhaps an apology might even be in order. She placed one foot on the metallic bleachers and began a climb to him. Aiden holstered his iPad. "There's something you should know," she began.

"Oh?" he said, curious.

"We've met before," she confessed.

"Yeah?"

"In school," she clarified, hesitating.

"Okay".

Teresa was looking to see if anything would jog his memory. But she thought to herself, *Honestly, why would it? Our encounter was so brief.* She continued stammering while stating her truth, "Did...my girlfriends...tell you any of this?"

"No," Aiden answered casually. "They just asked if I'd like to go on a blind date. That she's pretty, smart, and fun. And that her first name is Teresa."

The stadium lights suddenly shut off, automatic timer, leaving them bathed in August moonlight. Teresa looked up at the stadium lights then back down at Aiden, continuing her reveal. She hesitated, then shrugged. "Well... I'm Teresa." She offered her hand, with an attempt to further explain. "I'm Teresa..."

"Callahan" he interrupted. They both paused. Teresa looked puzzled. Aiden continued, "Your name is Teresa Callahan. It means 'bright headed', right?'" he added softly.

"Did my girlfriends tell you my last name?" Teresa asked, surprised, a second mystery for her today.

"No," he whispered.

She asked, "Then how did you..."

Again, she was interrupted. This time by Aiden's movement. He retrieved his leather wallet from his front pocket, reached in, and pulled out a thin paper that was aged with yellowing and creases. A receipt. An ATM receipt. He read from the paper, "Your name is Teresa Callahan and fifteen years ago you had forty-three dollars and eighteen cents in your Partners First Federal Credit Union checking account. He glanced at her, smiling. "I looked up your surname's meaning. It's kind of a hobby of mine."

Teresa stared at the receipt, her pulse quickening as the connection hit her. She couldn't believe that he'd kept the receipt. She looked again into his Irish green eyes, and the same trance-like state began to overtake her. "I kissed you," she murmured.

"Don't I know it?" he replied with a grin. "Actually, I'd call it 'making out.'"

She laughed, remembering her boldness from back then. The memory struck her hormones. She hadn't just kissed him. She'd pulled him into her audaciousness, like a tractor beam. He was right. She'd made out with him. But those times were so much more than kisses, now. They were enmeshed with familiarity that had ripened over the years, like perfectly aged wine. And that nervous energy, that wanting energy, had aged well into one fine vintage.

Teresa sat down beside him, her tush inadvertently crashing against his on impact with the bleachers. Her momentum in the drop had also inadvertently crashed her torso against him, as well. The feedback from the collisions echoed the firmness of his fit build. "Soccer guys stay in great shape", she thought. His "hotness" had compounded over the years: powerful legs, a thin abdominal region, and defined forearms that a sketch artist could use as a learning model. Teresa chuckled again with this realization. A sketch, after all, was what had guided her here this evening.

Though infatuation was still brewing within her, Teresa still felt that she needed to apologize. She began to drive in that direction when Aiden gently hushed her. His acceptance was even more bonding. "We were kids".

She shook her head in agreement, swallowing his gentle forgiveness. She looked at him, seeing her own reflection in those forest-green eyes and for the first time in a long time, knowing that she was truly seen. She realized that Elina had been right, that through all those previous trials, having Aiden there would have made navigating them so much easier.

"You've no idea how often I thought about you," she admitted softly.

"Me too," he replied, his brow furrowing.

She smirked when she remembered how she'd thought about him in more "poetic" ways, as well. And, whether it was hormones or the trust from knowing each other as kids, Teresa dipped her hand into the waters of bravery again, expanding on her statement. "No, like *thought* of you". She lowered her voice for emphasis, trying to allude to just when and how she had thought of him.

Had she revealed too much? She was beginning to feel those old feelings of moving a thousand miles per hour. The rush. Oh, God. Was he now going to be the one to run away? Her head was spinning. She braced herself when she heard him chuckle. Aiden shook his head in understanding, and softly huffed, "Me too."

The pause between them buzzed with energy. Teresa felt the rush of yesteryear pass through her, again, an internal wind of daringness and trust. In one smooth movement, she moved her hands to his face, and pressed her lips against him, again – finally.

~ ~

Teresa labeled his initial response at her daringness as "surprise", but a split second later he had adapted, parting his lips to receive her. He tasted the same as he had fifteen years ago, maybe even better, like aged wine from an artisan vintner. Aiden had added a counter move to this kiss, though. In a motion even more smooth than hers, he'd wrapped his arm around her waist, pulled her onto him, and stood up. His second arm secured her. He wasn't letting her go this time. Teresa wrapped her legs around him, reinforcing the idea. She wasn't letting go either.

Aiden's full lips grazed her neck. At first, they were simple, delicate pecks, a greeting to her soft neckline. But emotionally, she could sense that his hunger for her was expanding, and as it did, his lips took the lead. His soft tongue signed into the game, becoming a reliable teammate to his lips and when they found the sensitive spot just below her ear, the world tilted.

Desire surged through Teresa, leaving her lightheaded, as if she were being swept away by a warm, irresistible tide.

Without hesitation, Aiden descended the metal staircase with Teresa wrapped securely around him. She did not ask where they were headed - it didn't matter. She was with him. He moved with steady confidence, each step deliberate, never faltering. She floated in his arms, her body curled around his torso, as though the world existed only for them.

She was acutely aware of the intimate closeness between them, the way her most precious secret pressed against him - but none of this mattered. In that moment, she was drawing something from him, something she craved just as much. Because, with every step he took, she felt the ripples of his abdominals through the thin barrier of her panties. The sensation teased her, igniting fantasies of indulgence and a desire to ride those sculpted muscles to the edge of her sanity. This thought alone sent a flush of heat through her.

When Teresa had snapped out of her momentary fantasy, she found that Aiden had brought her to the soccer field. The grass remained warm, having sunned itself throughout the day and its professionally manicured tone resembled a heated carpet against her back. Their lips hadn't parted during the journey. Their tongues continued moving in a rhythm that left Teresa breathless. Her chest rose and fell with the weight of her desire.

Her hips lifted toward him instinctively, searching for the rub down again from his abs. Aiden arched his back, the hardness within his soccer shorts brushed against her. The sensation left her whispering a single, supportive word: "Damn".

He let out a breathless laugh, her desire reflected in his eyes. In a hurried manner, and huffing with his own desire, Aiden pushed himself onto his knees, then pulled his shirt from over his back. The full effect of his sculpted-ness sat before her, and "damn" was no longer a fitting depiction. Any new description would have to begin with the word, "Holy".

Teresa reached up for him, landing her fingertips on his abs and the backside of her elbow on her own treasure. Her admiration traced his abdominals along with her fingers, following their peaks and valleys as though she were committing them to memory. Their ripples excited her further. Her fingers channeled the energy of his powerful physique down her own forearm to the heart of her femininity. Her back arched forward, instinctively. She savored the feeling, closing her eyes.

Aiden guided her hand to his face. Teresa could feel her pussy fluttering with excitement when his full lips caressed her curious fingertips, then eventually pulled Teresa's ring finger into his mouth, sucking her. She felt the strength of those lips pull her finger inside of him. His green-eyed, predatory gaze fastened itself to the softness of her yielding glances. The wetness of his lips and tongue mirrored Teresa's own wetness. Her elbow continued to rest against herself, again transferring the energy from his lips and tongue directly to her.

Teresa knew that Aiden had a direct line of sight to her lower lips, but she no longer cared. She had waved the white flag of surrender long ago, the moment that he carried her, literally sweeping her off of her feet. In turn, she could see him being just as vulnerable as she glanced at the throb in his shorts, howling with excitement.

Aiden's teasing intensified, his lips pulled her finger in and out, his movements deliberate and laden with meaning. The sensuality of his actions magnified her hunger for him. She cupped her free fingers around his jaw, feeling the strength in his features. When he released her finger, his lips didn't stop; they transitioned seamlessly to the inside of her palm, then her wrist, each kiss leaving a trail of heat in its wake.

Aiden's lips followed the shadow of his exhales, kissing her wrist, then along her forearm, and continuing to slide forward. His breath was a warm whisper against her skin. But, that breath quickened with excitement when his lips rounded her shoulders, then lingered momentarily in the alley between her breasts. His teeth gently coaxed the surrender of their sundress covering. A swelling of want flushed through Teresa when his lips and strong tongue unveiled their intentions to the valley between her breasts, as well as her nipples. They lingered there momentarily before continuing their descent along her abdomen. Teresa's hips arched off the ground as anticipation swelled within her. Her fingers found his hair, tangling themselves in the wavy strands, grounding her in the storm of sensation.

When his lips reached their destination, Teresa's mind emptied. Thinking was no longer possible; all that remained was an overwhelming, aching need. Both hands gripped a fist full of his hair as his lips and tongue danced along her outer thigh, then ventured inward. His breath warmed her through the thin fabric of her panties, the teasing touch driving her wild. When his cheek rested against her, Teresa thought she might finish through her panties from the simple touch of masculine features resting against her.

She continued to massage her fingers through his hair. "Something to hold onto", she thought. Aiden's tongue outlined her folds through the fabric, sending waves of anticipating pleasure coursing through her. She gasped as the warm night air kissed her skin, and he had shifted her panties aside. His lips met hers, their connection raw and electric. She reached upward and pulled the top of her summer dress downward, fully exposing her breasts to the voyeuristic August night. Aiden's hands followed hers, cupping her breasts as his lips continued their teen-age make out session with her pussy.

The pace between them quickened. Teresa's back arched upward as Aiden's tongue slipped inside her, a breathless "Oh my God" escaping her lips. His movements were deliberate, his tongue exploring her with a fullness that made her toes curl. She was being fucked by Aiden's tongue. His mouth and hands worked in harmony, one teasing her breasts while the other anchored her, steadying her through the storm.

Two fingers gently pinched a nipple while, simultaneously, Aiden's mouth had moved to introduce himself to Teresa's clit. With a gentlemanly bow, his tongue politely requested a dance with her. Knowing that such a request would inevitably take her over the edge, Teresa's clit curtsied in formal acceptance. As a gentleman, his tongue paraded around her permitter, flashing features like a peacock. Her clit bathed in the attention. Then swiftly, and seemingly inadvertently, his tongue strolled across the top. Teresa's back curled with excitement, as she moaned, "Yes."

His movements were both overwhelming and precise. His tongue danced around her, teasing and coaxing, until finally brushing over her with deliberate pressure. Teresa gasped, her body reacting instinctively, her hips rising to meet him. Aiden's hunger for her was palpable, every movement of his lips and tongue reflected his desire.

His hands continued massaging and steadying her via her breasts. Teresa appreciated hearing the moans of enjoyment Aiden emanated from tasting her. The reverberations of his voice gently shook her clit even more.

Like an antebellum dance, his tongue handed her clitoris off to his lips, another gentleman who bowed in introduction. This gentleman was a much more direct dancer. Not Fred Astaire, but more Patrick Swayze - Dirty Dancing. His lips seized her clit, fully taking her into his mouth. Just as Aiden had done with her finger, his tongue pushed her out, while his lips sucked her back in. She was experiencing the full lip and tongue, push-pull action that men receive from a blow job. This was new. She cherished the realization that her clit was inside his mouth, sucking her.

On one stroke of her clit being pulled fully into Aiden's mouth, he held her inside him, while gently reintroducing his tongue. She moaned with his rhythm. His tongue became more daring, more fluid like in his movements, like a private lap dance. And with the curtain of his lips drawing privacy around her clit, his tongue could swell around her however he pleased.

She felt him release her breast and reposition one hand under her backside. He was trying, desperately, to pull more of her into him. His observed and genuine hunger for her radiated through Teresa's body. She pushed his head into her while, coincidentally, his second hand presented a strong finger. Her body swooned with the combined wetness of his mouth and her nature.

Her crescendo, just beyond reach. Aiden's finger joined in the seduction, presenting himself just outside her lips before easily sliding in and resting against her north wall. The additional pressure, combined with his lips sucking her clit into his mouth, and his tongue frolicking about, flooded her. Ripples and pulses accumulated. She voluntarily followed her body's leap. Her toes curled. The moan of release echoed off the stadium walls. Her pussy pulsed. Then, her leg. Ripples flooded through her. Ripple after ripple reminding her of Aiden's abs. The ripples morphed into waves. Overtaking waves. He increased the internal pressure, literally pushing the waves out of her.

They continued. Teresa wondered if they would stop. Each ripple and wave combo lingered. Backed by another. But, eventually, the timing between them began to increase. What began as split-second responses, eventually downshifted into heartbeats, and before long dissipated into momentary aftershocks.

With her thighs draped over his full shoulders and Aiden's warm cheek resting against her wetness, Teresa basked in her nest of afterglow. Her hands reclaimed their position, with her fingers running through his hair, massaging him. Wonderment, and appreciation blanketed them. Silence enveloped them, broken only by the shared rhythm of their breaths.

Finally, Aiden spoke, his tone light but carrying an undercurrent of mischief. "I have something very important to ask you."

"Oh God", Teresa considered. Reasoning had not yet fully returned to her cognitive abilities. "What on earth could this possibly be?" She paused to consider all that had occurred through their years. How she'd reacted when she was a kid. What she was missing out on. Where was he emotionally?

He fortified the tension that she tortured herself with by saying, "It's kind of important".

With no alternative, she relented, "Okay. Ask away."

He comically stumbled, "Can I...get your number...finally?" He then paused, gazed at her directly, and burst into laughter. She instinctively smiled with relief and could not help but follow him. She lay there virtually naked. Satisfied. Vulnerable. Their laughter grew together into shared bellows. Their amusement echoed off the stadium walls and faded into the August night sky as evidence of their undeniable chemistry.

More tales lie in wait, sealed in letters only the bold may open.
Join Morgan's circle for exclusive content at
www.TheKnightOfRomance.com

Art Appreciation Day

Dark, intense, and impossible to forget, the first sip of this story strikes with a bite - a rush of adrenaline fueled by tension and temptation. As the story opens up, velvety layers of dark suggestions mix with rich and unspoken desires, creating a slow-burning heat. A whisper of smoky danger lingers in the background, softened by playful spice - an unexpected thrill that keeps you craving more. And just as the final drop fades, the finish lingers, bittersweet and intoxicating, a taste that refuses to let go.

Suggested Pairings

Wine: Vietti Barolo Castiglione

Cocktail: Negroni, with a spicy twist.

Coffee: Italian Espresso with Dark Chocolate

Zero Proof: Blood Orange & Chili Spritz

To stir, shake, or savor like the characters do, visit
www.*TheKnightOfRomance*.com for each drink's recipe.

"Dammit. Fucking GO!" Erin growled, smacking the steering wheel with her palm. The horn gave a weak honk in protest, as if exhausted by her outburst. She leaned forward, glaring at the old Toyota truck that had cut her off for the third time. "You moron!" she added for good measure.

"What is wrong with you?" her sister's voice crackled through the earbuds, a mix of curiosity and concern.

"This damn Toyota keeps blocking me. Every time I try to pass, he swerves over like he owns the road," Erin grumbled, her knuckles whitening around the steering wheel. The pickup truck ahead sported a patchwork of obnoxious bumper stickers, but one stood out in bold, peeling letters: *Cletus Rules!*

"You wanna call me back?" her sister asked.

"No. Stay on the line. Keep me calm. I'm not about to rear-end some ass clown," Erin huffed, tapping her fingers on the wheel like a frustrated drumbeat.

Her sister chuckled softly. "Alright, then. Tell me about him."

"Cletus?"

"No, you idiot," her sister laughed. "Marco."

"Oh." Erin's tone softened instantly, her mind shifting from road rage to something much warmer. "Right. Marco." She rolled her eyes at herself, shaking her head. "I thought you meant the ass wipe in front of me."

"Please, tell me you didn't just confuse the guy you're crushing on with 'Cletus Rules,'" her sister teased.

"Shut up." Erin smirked, the tension loosening as she took a breath. "Anyway... oh my god, Marco is *so* cute. Like, you don't even understand. I'm almost at his café right now, and I'm dying."

"Well," her sister said, "don't let Cletus ruin your vibe."

"Believe me," Erin grinned, her heart racing for a different reason now, "nothing's ruining this."

"You're doing a drive-by?" her sister accused, her voice dripping with amusement.

"Noooooo," Erin replied, drawing out the denial in a way that made it sound even more suspicious. Then, with a sigh, she confessed, "Okay, fine. I'm just... checking on him."

Her sister snorted. "Oh, sure. You think he's just going to *happen* to be outside, wiping down tables or something?"

"You never know," Erin said, shrugging as she inched forward in bumper-to-bumper traffic. "If I ever friggin' get there."

The gridlocked street was testing her patience. But nothing could dim her determination to catch a glimpse of Marco. He was the perfect excuse to stop by the café for a cappuccino and one of his heavenly pastries, or maybe the other way around. "Marco's Italian Café" a coffee house owned by Marco Bellucci, former Formula One racing driver turned café owner. He served authentic Italian coffee and French pastries so rich and decadent that Erin had once described them to her sister as "palette porn."

Twice a week, she made excuses to visit. She always struck a balance, making sure her visits were frequent enough to show interest but spaced out enough to avoid crossing the border into "Stalkerville." The flirty chats with Marco behind the counter were her personal highlight, a mix of charm, laughter...and hope.

Her sister broke the brief silence. "You know what they say about those guys, right?"

Erin blinked, glancing at the traffic ahead. "What guys?"

"Duhhhhhh, race car drivers," her sister replied with exaggerated patience, as if this should be obvious.

"Oh god," Erin sighed, bracing herself. "No. What do they say?", her curiosity piqued.

Her sister hesitated, her voice dropping as if someone might overhear. "That they can... ya know."

"Ya know what?" Erin pressed, glancing toward the traffic as her car inched forward.

"Like... satisfy themselves," her sister said, pausing just long enough for Erin's mind to race before adding, "while driving."

Erin nearly choked on her laugh. "Nuh-uh! No way."

"Yeah, huh," her sister insisted, giggling. "I guess the speed turns them on or something."

"I don't believe it." But even as she said it, a tiny spark of intrigue flickered inside her. The mental image of Marco behind the wheel, adrenaline coursing through him, was far more thrilling than she'd like to admit.

Her sister wasn't letting it go. "That's just what they say."

Erin shook her head, smirking. "Well, if it's true, then I really need to see what this guy can do off the track."

Erin doubted she'd ever get the chance to find out the truth about Marco. His signals were a maddening maze of mixed messages, and it was beginning to feel like an impossible puzzle. Every time she entered his café, the bell above the door would clang, announcing her arrival like fate itself wanted to give her a shot. And each time, Marco would look up, lock eyes with her, and smile - that devastating smile.

His was not just any smile, either. Marco's was one flanked by cheekbones that seemed carved by the gods and anchored by a jawline so sharp it could cut glass. And if his smile did not disarm her, his resting expression would, somewhere between boyish innocence and the kind of danger that sent shivers down Erin's spine. Add to that the mop of jet-black hair that flopped in perfect disarray with every turn of his head, and Erin found herself thinking the same thing every woman did when they saw it: *Why is that luxurious hair wasted on a man?*

But beauty could only get her so far. As much as she admired him, her frustration was mounting. This was not the first time that she'd shaved her legs for a fucking cup of coffee. She silently cursed her own optimism. She did not come to Marco's for pastries or caffeine. She came to gauge his interest. Was he just being polite or was he playing some cruel game of red light - green light, and Erin couldn't figure out how to win?

Was he married? Did he have a girlfriend? Was he gay? None of these seemed likely based on her many café stakeouts. But there was no denying that she was stuck in neutral. "What's it gonna take to get this thing in gear?" she wondered as she tapped her fingers against the steering wheel.

Marco was not just a man, he was a puzzle, one of those complicated 3D ones that only came in boxes labeled *1,000 pieces, along with a message from the manufacturer reading "Good Luck!"* And right now, luck was not on her side. She thought back to how simple things had been when she was a kid. If she liked a boy, she didn't sit around analyzing every smile and glance. She'd pass him a quick note:

I like you.
Do you like me?

Yes   or   No
(Please circle one.)

Maybe she should bring that strategy out of retirement. That might be faster than this agonizing game of "guess if he's flirting or just polite."

The odd thing about Marco was that he had a way of making Erin feel wanted without saying much at all. Their conversations, though casual and brief, had a way of lingering in her thoughts long after she left the café. His charm was subtle, but stuck to her like honey, sweet and slow. Should she just take the plunge and give him her number? Her Snap? At this point, she'd even settle for a LinkedIn connection. She snorted at the thought.

That's when she remembered the poster she'd seen at the BMW dealership earlier: *"Let's get this thing in gear!"* She had laughed out loud at it then, and she was laughing again now. "Yeah, Marco," she whispered to herself. "Let's."

But no one on the street was in gear today. And then there was Cletus, the Toyota driver who had somehow made this his personal mission to ruin her afternoon. His obnoxious bumper stickers glared at her, as if mocking her lack of control. All she wanted was to make the last two blocks to Marco's café, but those two blocks might as well have been miles. Every time she tried to switch lanes, Cletus cut her off again, testing her patience and sanity.

The street had turned into a crawling herd of steel cattle, moving one hoof at a time. *Stop. Go. Stop. Go.* Erin's patience had sputtered out miles ago, and the polite little honk of her BMW's horn was doing nothing to ease her frustration. She tapped it again, harder this time, using it like an emotional pressure release valve.

Finally, she made it within sight of Marco's café, just in time to catch a brief glimpse of him walking inside with a backpack slung over his shoulder. Her heart skipped. Was he leaving? Had he forgotten something? She craned her neck, but before she could get another look, she came to a sudden, jarring halt.

Cletus was not moving.

His truck was parked dead in the middle of the lane. Erin's eyes widened as she watched him throw the vehicle into PARK and swing the driver's door open.

"Oh my god," Erin whispered, her voice rising in panic as she spoke into her earbuds. "He's completely stopped."

"What!?!" her sister asked, her concern evident.

"No, seriously. He just put it in PARK, and he's, I think he... HOLY SHIT! HE'S GETTING OUT OF HIS TRUCK."

"NO!" her sister yelled, her voice cracking with disbelief.

"Stay on the phone," Erin pleaded, her heart thundering in her chest. She watched as Cletus slammed the door of his 70s-style pickup, the metallic clang echoing like a warning shot through the street. His boots crunched over roadside gravel and trampled weeds, his gait steady and determined like a confederate soldier advancing into battle.

Erin shrank back into her seat, her fingers trembling as she cracked the window just enough for her voice to slip through. Her plan? Play dumb. Play docile. Anything to avoid escalating the situation. *Rednecks are notorious for road rage,* she thought grimly. *Any rage, really.*

"I'm okay," she squeaked, her voice small. "Sorry. Accidentally had my hand stuck on the horn while trying to fix my seat belt."

But Cletus wasn't buying the excuse. He strolled up to her BMW, planted one dirty hand on the roof, his fingers curling over the sleek paint like Erin's car was his to own. His eyes narrowed, his jaw clenched, and then, without warning, he spat, "What's your fuckin' problem, bitch?"

Erin's jaw dropped. The word hit her like a slap across the face. She felt the sting before she could fully process it.

Her sister's voice exploded through her earbuds. "He did NOT just call you a bitch."

Erin swallowed hard, her throat dry, as Cletus leaned in closer. His breath was hot, fogging her window while his voice was low and venomous. "I asked you," he hissed again, "what the fuck is your problem?"

Erin remained silent, her eyes locked forward, refusing to meet Cletus's glare. Fear tightened its grip around her chest as his insults escalated, each word slicing deeper. She could feel herself shrinking under the weight of his aggression. And then, to make things worse, Marco appeared in the doorway of his café.

Her heart sank when she spotted him. Marco stood there, as effortlessly handsome as ever, his smile radiant with warmth. Then, with a flourish, he waved. His eyes were alight with an unspoken *glad to see you*, a silent embrace across the space between them. He had not yet registered the chaos unfolding with Cleutus. Erin's face flushed, a mixture of embarrassment and dread creeping over her. She peeked at him through the corner of her eye, wincing as if her shame were physically dragging her down.

Marco's smile faded as his gaze shifted to Cletus, who was now practically shouting, veins bulging as he launched another verbal grenade. "I should've known that some *cunt* driving a BMW can't even buy American."

Erin froze, the word sending a shockwave through her system. Her sister's voice exploded in her ear, outraged. "He DID NOT just call you a *cunt!*"

Before Erin could respond, a thunderous voice cut through the chaos.

"HEEEY!" Marco's shout rumbled across the street, loud and commanding. Both Erin and Cletus jolted as Marco stormed forward, his posture firm, unflinching. His steps were purposeful, his face a mixture of fury and focus. "What are you doing stopping traffic? In front of *my* café?"

Marco's words hit like a fighter jet, fast and unrelenting. His thick Italian accent added weight to every syllable, making it impossible to ignore. "Move your truck," he ordered, his arms flailing to punctuate his words. Cletus tried to fire back, barking, "Mind your business, asshole!"

Marco did not flinch. He didn't even blink. "*Asshole?* You want me to mind business? *Thiz IS my bizness!* You are blocking *MY* bizness." His words came sharp, like precision-guided missiles, each statement landing perfectly. "She'z customer. You are a *pezzo di merda*" - a piece of shit.

Erin's eyes widened. She could barely keep up with Marco's rapid-fire insults, but the sheer speed and force of them left her stunned and impressed. Cletus, on the other hand, was visibly thrown off balance, retreating step by step toward his truck as Marco continued his verbal assault.

"I am making a police call into you!" Marco shouted, his arms still flailing as if he could physically shove Cletus back with the force of his words. "You are wanting American? You drive *Toyota*, moron."

Erin's lips curled into the smallest smile. *That's exactly what I was thinking.*

Marco paused for just a moment, catching his breath, and Cletus tried to seize the opening. "Crazy, European fuck," he spat, lobbing the insult like a last-ditch grenade.

Big mistake.

Marco's eyes darkened, absorbing the insult like fuel for the fire. He repurposed it instantly, turning it into a weapon of his own. "That'z right! You want crazy? You come to me!" His voice grew louder, fiercer. "I am making you lick my balls! Get out of zere. Go! Get! Get, *little dog!* Get!"

Cletus's glare remained fixed on Marco, but he had no more weapons to fire. He climbed back into his truck, threw it into gear, and squealed his tires in defeat as he sped off, leaving behind nothing but the smell of burnt rubber and the sound of Marco's victory echoing down the street.

Erin sat frozen for a moment, processing what had just happened. Marco had taken the ground, and she was still catching her breath.

Grinning from ear to ear, Erin guided her car into an open roadside parking space right next to Marco. Despite the heated exchange that had just unfolded, Marco's demeanor was completely unshaken. He stood there like nothing had happened - calm, collected, and as warm as a gardener watering his flowers.

"Where did *that* come from?" she asked, still marveling at how quickly he had transformed into a force of nature moments ago.

He shrugged casually, his lips curling into a soft smile. "Ahhhh, he is ignorance. We have zem in Italy, too. I seez zem all da time in racing. He'z nothing."

Erin couldn't help but admire how easily he dismissed Cletus as if he were no more significant than a fly buzzing around. And in that same moment, the inspiration solidified into something more when Marco's gaze softened, and he tilted his head ever so slightly. "How are you?" he asked, the sincerity in his voice caused Erin's heart to stumble.

"Good. I - I - I was just coming to see you," she blurted, her cheeks flushing as the words left her mouth. *What did I just say?* It was a slip, an unfiltered truth she hadn't meant to reveal, and she instantly regretted it.

But then Marco's eyes lit up, and his smile widened with genuine excitement. "Really? To see me?"

Her sister's voice exploded in her ear. "Uh-ohhhhhhh."

"'Scuse me," Erin mumbled, motioning to Marco with an apologetic smile. She quickly tapped her earbuds and whispered, "I'll call you back," before selecting "End Call." As soon as the line disconnected, she turned her full attention back to Marco.

"Are you leaving?" she asked, trying to sound casual, as if she had not just declared her intentions to come see him.

"Yes," Marco replied, gesturing toward the café. "I have not clozed, but am leaving ze café in my hostess's hands. She is capable."

Erin could barely focus on the content of his words. The way he pronounced every syllable with that rich Italian accent, slightly broken yet so precise, sent her into a soft, swooning haze. She could feel herself getting lost in it, the way he turned even the simplest sentence into something musical.

Sensing her chance, Erin flashed a warm smile and asked, "Do you want a ride?"

Marco's brows lifted slightly, and a playful smirk spread across his face. "I have not told you where I am going. Maybe I am going to an unzafe neighborhood... full of pickup trucks and rednecks who will find your prezence offensive."

Erin's stomach did a nervous flip with laughter. She felt her cheeks heat up from being called out, but she recovered quickly. "Ahhhhh, yeah. I grew up there," she teased, surprising herself with the witty comeback. Internally, she gave herself a high-five for keeping her cool despite the flurry of nerves swirling inside her.

In truth, this wasn't about offering him a ride. Erin just wanted to be near him. There was something about Marco's presence that soothed her, grounding her in a way she hadn't expected. Maybe that was why she spent so much time at his café, she reasoned. She wasn't attracted to just his looks, though they were undeniably magnetic. But Marco had a way of making Erin feel like her best, boldest self. When she was near him, her confidence grew, her horizons seemed wider, and her understanding of the world around her deepened. *How is that even possible,* she wondered, glancing at him.

A lull settled between them, not awkward but charged, as if the universe had hit pause. Their eyes met, and for a moment, neither of them spoke, but everything they wanted to say hung in the air between them. Then, suddenly, Erin's stomach made itself known with a loud, embarrassing rumble that practically screamed, *HANGRY.*

She laughed, breaking the silence, and took the moment to throw out a casual alternative. "Wanna grab lunch?"

Marco's face lit up, his enthusiasm immediate. "YES!" he replied, his voice full of warmth. "BBQ? After chatting with redneck perzon, I am hungry for BBQ. You?"

Erin giggled, her eyes sparkling as she met his gaze. "Yes. BBQ sounds great." Her inner dialogue could not help but finish the thought: *Austin has the best BBQ. AND... he likes me.* Her heart swelled with possibility. Today would not be just about lunch, but a step toward something real, something worth chasing.

Marco stepped toward the passenger door as if to open it for himself but hesitated, his hand resting on the handle. "One queshon," he said with a hint of charm. "Do you mind if I am driving? It relaxez me."

Erin snickered, the last remnants of tension from the Cletus encounter had dissolved. The idea of Marco at the wheel felt more like a gift than a request. "All yours," she replied, unbuckling her seatbelt and making the awkward crawl across the car to the passenger seat.

She tried to keep her skirt from riding up over the stick shift, but in her heart, she didn't mind that Marco caught a brief glimpse of her thigh as she shifted into place. She had always been self-conscious about her chest, but her legs? Those she knew were a strong point. As she shimmied into the seat, she masked her awkward movement with conversation. "Plus... it's not every day that you get to be chauffeured by a race car driver."

Marco opened the driver's side door, tossing his backpack into the back seat before sliding in with the kind of effortless grace that made her stomach flutter. "Dis is true," he agreed, his accent making the words sound sweeter. Then, with a cocky grin that matched his tone, he corrected her. "But not 'race car driver' - *Formula One* driver."

Erin tilted her head and raised an eyebrow. "There's a difference?"

Marco laughed softly, his hands mimicking a giant steering wheel as he mocked the idea. "Race car drivers, zat is what Cletus watches. Vroom, vroom, in a big circle. Again...and again."

Erin couldn't help but giggle as he exaggerated the motion like he was driving a monster truck in slow motion.

"Formula One driver," he continued, shifting from playful to poetic, "is lover. Lover of speed. Lover of life." His fingers pressed together, like he was describing a fine Italian meal. "Is not about Vroom, vroom. Is about movement, precision. Passion."

His words hung in the air like a melody, captivating Erin more than she anticipated. She was mesmerized by the way he spoke, not just what he said, but how he said it, each syllable rolling smoothly off his tongue like a poet's. And then there was his smile. God, that smile. Warm, inviting, and utterly disarming.

Erin could feel her heart beating just a little faster as she thought to herself, *Lover of life, huh? That's exactly the kind of energy I need.* Erin surrendered, "Well then, take me away Formula One driver", as she sank back into her seat.

The phone rang. Erin's sister. She answered, "I'm okay. Call you back later." She quickly hung up and placed the interrupting device in a cup holder. When doing so, Erin completed a full body scan of Marco in the seat beside her. He seemed to melt into that position like liquid metal that had dissolved into a smooth weld. He was one with the vehicle. His poise percolated with more pep, and a raging smile ripened before her eyes. He and the car, the two, were a natural fit.

Erin's eyes naturally traced the outline of Marco's body against the leather. Ordinary drivers do not sit with such effortless grace, poised like a statue that embodies both alertness and comfort. Marco's knee was slightly bent with the same angle duplicated as his arms. His shoulders instinctively pressed themselves into the seat back. His lap, loose to accommodate quick turns, while his - *Wait! Was he?* Erin swore she noticed a lump in Marco's groin region. *Was he getting hard,* she silently wondered. Erin had to look away for a moment before glancing again for confirmation. Was the car doing that to him? Was it her? Was it a combination? Maybe her sister had been right. Either way, the thought sparked an inspirational response in Erin.

"Buckled up?", Marco asked.

"Uh-huh", Ering gasped. Anticipation flowed through her in two waves, one for the ride from a formula one race car driver, and the second from what she just witnessed in Marco's lap.

"I am going to show you what your ***pussy*** can do", he said.

"WHAT?!?", Erin shot back.

Marco innocently replied, "The car. I am going to show you what your *beamer* can do. Is this not correct English?" Erin had mistaken what he'd said, replacing *"beamer"* for *"pussy"*. She laughed, also remembering Julia Roberts saying something almost identical to Richard Gere in Pretty Woman.

"Ohhhhhhhh", she snickered, a little relieved but more disappointed. "Pussy would have been much more interesting", she hummed to herself.

Marco leaned over slightly and whispered with a mischievous grin, "Start your engines."

Erin chuckled softly, but inside her mind, her response was much more charged. *I'm already started,* she thought, her pulse quickening.

When Marco turned the key, the engine purred to life with a deep, resonant growl - a nearly romantic sound Erin had not heard from her car before. The vehicle did not sound like a machine anymore; but more like a living, breathing sculpture, designed to thrill and overwhelm the senses.

"Ready?" he asked, his tone carrying that confident edge she found impossible to resist.

"Red'..." She barely got the word out before Marco punched the accelerator, and her breath sank to the back of her throat as the car launched forward like a slingshot. Excitement surged through her, shooting adrenaline that raced through her veins. Her internal critic scrambled for footing. *Damn, I think he might actually be a professional driver.* There was no doubt now, this was not just a man who simply knew how to drive; this was a man who *lived* for it.

Strapped in tight, with no room to move, Erin savored the thrill. The force of acceleration pressed her back into her leather seat, her body surrendering to the car's power. But speed and acceleration weren't the only thing sending her pulse racing, the lingering miscommunication about the word "pussy" buzzed in her mind like a teasing echo. Combined with the pressure of the seat holding her captive and the seductive growl of the engine, Erin felt the subtle, unmistakable undertone of wetness blooming between her thighs.

Her breathing quickened, but she kept her peripheral gaze on Marco, who was effortlessly navigating the road, his calm poise only adding to the tension swirling inside her. *This is not just a drive,* she realized. *This is an experience.*

The sentiment intensified as Erin stole another glance at Marco. His dark, wavy hair tousled slightly from the breeze slipping through the slightly cracked window, and his mischievous eyes held a spark that effortlessly complimented his high-performance body. But beyond the physical allure that naturally drew attention wherever he went, there was something deeper. Something intangible. A presence. Calm, smooth, and soft, like an emotionally intelligent artist searching for his perfect canvas.

Only Marco's canvas was not stretched across a wooden frame. No. His canvas lived on the edge of 200 mph. His art was not brushstrokes, but precision, control, and daring finesse behind the wheel. And now, Erin sat quietly in his studio, relishing every second of watching him create.

In mere moments, they had busted through the frustrating two-mile stretch of traffic that had boxed her in earlier. The freeway stretched wide in front of them, virtually empty, the open road inviting them forward like a blank page waiting to be filled with their story.

"Where's the traffic?" Erin asked, the question slipping out as she realized how effortlessly they had broken free.

Marco's pause was deliberate. His grin, amusing and cocky, "Behind us".

"Ohhhhhhh," Erin breathed, a sense of awe and admiration wrapped inside the sound.

She knew they had long since surpassed a hundred miles per hour, but she never glanced at the speedometer. This was not just a car ride, but something more, something untethered from the ordinary. This felt like flight, as if they were already at cruising altitude, gliding effortlessly through the night.

And then came the familiar, that warmth of comfort and ease she always felt around Marco, swelled inside her like a tide. He offered more than easy conversation; he radiated a kind of comfort that made her feel utterly unguarded, free - like she could say or do anything without judgement. The kind of comfort where you sink into your couch with a glass of pinot noir, wrapped in an oversized flannel and thigh-high leg warmers, while the fire crackles low in the background.   That rare, intoxicating feeling where everything is exactly as it should be, and the world hums just right with the gentle lull of a wine buzz.

The thoughts were as intoxicating as her vehicle's speed. Marco was the perfect mixture of exhilaration and safety. The memory of the earlier miscommunication - the word "pussy" - flashed through her mind again, bringing a small, amused smirk to her lips. *Damn, if only.*

Still, the speed alone was doing his job. The hum of the engine, the pressure of the seat, and Marco's confident grip on the wheel all combined into something electric. The sensation of arousal lingered, teasing her. Erin let out a soft chuckle, shaking her head at herself, *Not sure I could get off with it, though,* she thought, *but damn, it is close.*

Marco's keen perception picked up on Erin's wondering thoughts. He exhaled, a low, amused chuckle following it. "There'z something on your minds?", he asked.

"Nope," Erin quipped without hesitation, amusement dancing in her voice.

Silence hung in the cockpit for a moment as the engine sang to them outside. Marco perked his lips, smiled and replied, "I am calling bullshit."

Erin shifted slightly in her seat, a flush of warmth spreading across her chest and cheeks, "You can tell what's on my mind?"

His response was slow, but playful. "Okay. So, somezhings is NOT on your mind?", he questioned, then glanced over at Erin's suspicious eyes.

Erin paused, "Well", then continued "I've got a question about you guys. But I'm afraid to ask".

Marco's silence demonstrated patience, elevating Erin's trust. He simply sat there, attentive, racing the two of them at remarkable speeds. The world blurred into comfortable streaks of light and motion, dissolving into the periphery, leaving only the two of them suspended in their own secret rhythm. Erin felt the exhilaration coil around her, a delicious intoxication born of movement and escape. They were ten steps ahead of the entire world, yet utterly unhurried. The thought sent a slow, smoldering heat through her, a spark of desire flickering to life, impossible to ignore. Her phone buzzed again. The display read, "Sister". She ignored it. But the phone spawned the idea to push the embarrassment for her curiosity onto someone else. Her nearly drunken state fused with her yearning to be touched and summoned her courage to ask.

"Sooooooo, my sister and I were talking one day," she began, drawing out the words. "Annnddd," Erin hesitated, fumbling, "we were talking about race car drivers. And *she* said... no! *I* heard -" She stammered again, flustered. "No! *She* heard, sorry." The hesitation was back, creeping in like an old habit.

"Heard what?", Marco replied, his voice playing with a suggestive tone.

Erin paused one final time. The nerves were back, fluttering around like butterflies on steroids, but she blurted out her half-baked inquiry, "That speed turns you guys on."

The air between them held its breath, waiting for Marco's reply.

"Well sure", he confidently beamed, allowing the confirmation to sink in before continuing, "Why do you think we drive? Your career does not excite you?"

Erin realized her point required clarification, "No, Like REALLY turns you on...". She could not believe what she was about to say. Her words unfolded slowly, "Like, Or...gasm...level turn on".

Marco did not hesitate, "Ahhh", he said, "So you want to know if the rumorz are true. If race car driver can cum while driving". His relaxed bluntness over word choice was freeing to Erin.

"Well, sure", she asserted.

A pause lingered between them, stretching as Marco smoothly navigated the turn. "Well, sure," he finally said, his voice easy. "Anyone cans, not just race car driverz."

"What!?!", Erin jumped.

"Anyone cans," he stressed, then added with a slight smirk, "Well, almost anyone."

"How do you figure?", Erin asked.

"Is easy. Is when you livez on zee edge of control. That edge? That is where life happens. We feelz most alive on zat edge. And, when you feels alive, you feels turned on. So. When you are actually on zee edge of control, you are more than half-wayz there. You are automatically turned onz. You zee the same things when people come backs from war, or survive being mugged. They feels appreciation for beings alive. They are turned on."

Erin's body betrayed her. Heat unfurled beneath her skin as she listened. She had to admit, there was something seductive in his words, the promise of surrender, or abandoning thought until only sensation remained, raw and electric. Her pulse quickened, drawn into the intoxicating allure of his words. *Spoken like a true artist*, she mused, the thought laced with both admiration and anticipation.

Yet, in raising the topic, had she unwittingly exposed herself? The thought unsettled her - had Marco's reasoning laid bare the depth of her desire, the way being lost in this moment with him had begun to burn deep inside her? She acknowledged that his reasoning was backed by pretty sound logic, maybe even science, but that didn't make it any easier to accept. Her ego bristled, reluctant to yield. "Not me" she deflected, masking the heat beneath a smirk. "That sounds like some Italian guy bullshit to me", she kidded while swooning inside.

His voice carried the quiet ease of someone who met life with gentle acceptance, "Okay", he replied. No counter argument. No protest. No objection, just a simple acknowledgment of Erin's words, whether he believed them or not. He let them stand, unchallenged, as if granting her the space to believe them herself. Again, creating more trust in him.

The road stretched endlessly ahead, while the smoldering weight of his words thickened, slow and golden, like warm honey. Erin felt as if they were already soaring - suspended somewhere between reality and a fantasy she had not yet dared to name. The steady hum of the engine, the low vibrations beneath her, and the quiet gravity of Marco's presence wove together, intoxicating and heady, a temptation she could easily lose herself in.

Marco reached for Erin's hand. Her breath shivered, suspended in the charged space between them. As his strong, warm fingers wove effortlessly through hers, Erin's heart stuttered. The moment was beginning to become overwhelming - an intoxicating blend of speed, safety, playful conversation, and now his touch. Marco raised her hand to his lips. *Oh, those full and enticing lips.* He teased each of her fingertips with a feather-light kiss before his lower lip cradled her knuckles. Erin felt a spark reaching into her core.

His gaze flicked to hers, a quiet appreciation flickering in his eyes, as if savoring the unspoken energy between them.

"Do youz trust me?", Marco asked, his voice a whisper against the engine purring and the road humming.

Her breath stuttered, her voice softer now, laced with something she could not quite contain. But she was back to being honest.

"Yes.", her response floated like fog into the chasm of anticipation.

Slowly, almost reverently, Marco lowered Erin's hand from his lips, guiding it gently to rest upon her knee. His own hand lingered atop hers, warm, steady - a silent claim. Their eyes met, a knowing smile passing between them, laced with something deeper, something unspoken. And then, as if her body had answered before her mind could catch up, her legs shifted, parting just slightly. He now knew. And Erin knew that he knew - just how much she wanted him.

With quiet certainty, Marco guided Erin's hand along the smooth plane of her inner thigh, the touch a slow revelation. She felt the whisper of fabric from her skirt lifting, surrendering to the moment. Her legs had already blabbed about her true desire and instinctively yielded to the unspoken rhythm between them. Marco's hand led her's further, until her fingertips found the soft curve beneath lace panties, where heat pulsed, velvet-rich and undeniable. A shiver traced her spine as she felt the sultry dampness gathering, the delicate bloom of her own longing pressed against her own touch while Marco's hand remained atop hers, mere millimeters away.

Marco's sculpted forearm settled against the stick shift of her BMW, a casual yet deliberate placement. But now, he had created a charged connection, a silent current bridging the pulse between Erin's legs to the hum of the engine, with Marco's forearm and fingers serving as their ambassador. A slow tremor unfurled within her, anticipation pooling low and deep as Marco let the moment stretch, drawing out the tension with the practiced ease of a man who understood the weight of such power.

With that same precision, Marco gently and momentarily pushed in the clutch, which raised the vehicle's RPMs. The vibrations raced through the stick shift, across Marco's forearm, through his fingers and stirred Erin. "Oh my God," she gasped, leaning forward as the intensity hit her, unexpected and exhilarating.

The engine purred, but beneath its restraint, she could sense something deeper, untamed power, coiled and waiting to be unleashed. A shiver ran down her spine as she realized this was only the beginning. There was so much more, perhaps more than she could ever handle. She bit her lip, trying to compose herself as the car surged forward.

After catching her breath, she whispered, "Do it again."

Marco did not hesitate. He adjusted their hands, pressing them directly against the damp fabric of her panties, the heat radiating through them. Erin was sure that Marco could now feel her wetness. With deliberate precision, he teased the throttle once more. The vibration magnified, shooting through her body like an unreachable desire. Erin's hips instinctively pushed forward, her breath catching in her throat as she gasped through the intensity. The sensation was addictive. She craved more.

"Again," she murmured, her voice dripping with need.

Marco remained effortlessly in control, his hands commanding both her pleasure and the vehicle with mastery. The world outside blurred, fading into insignificance as he played with the dance between the throttle and clutch. Each subtle shift and surge pulled her closer to the brink, tightening the coil inside her.

Her gasps melted into soft, desperate moans. In a flash, she withdrew her own hand. Marco's fingers landed directly against Erin's wetness. Unable to hold back, and wanting his direct touch, she had given him full access to her pussy. She reached for his face, her fingers delicately tracing the sharp lines of his jaw, silently pleading. His hand pressed firmly against her lips, grounding her in the moment, while the vehicle hummed beneath them like an extension of his desire. The vibrations flowed through the seat, hitting her rhythmically. They felt like beats. This now felt like thrusting. He was having her. Erin was being fucked. But she was being fucked by a man's art...a man's appreciation of life. The swirling of this abstract idea pushed Erin to the edge.

Her pussy lips swelled, fully open, accepting everything that the moment could give her. The restraint of the seat belt heightened her desire, creating a push-pull dynamic that only intensified the ache. She wanted to thrust forward, to meet his fingers, but the restraint held her back, driving her wild.

Her body trembled, desperate for release as the world spun into ecstasy. She moaned through her whispered plea, "Make me cum."

The thrusts and vibrations never faltered, each one rippling through her body with a force that made her tremble. Outside, the world blurred into a forgotten backdrop, speed and motion melting away into the singular, explosive moment unfolding inside her. She arched her back, chasing that inevitable crash through the finish line, her breath quickening as she swore she could hear the roar of an invisible crowd along with the sounds of rushing air, the hum of the engine, and the desperate rhythm of her pulse.

"Pleeeease," she whimpered, her voice fragile and pleading. Another thrust.

"Make..." another surge.

"Me...." another jolt, relentless.

Marco mercifully drifted the passenger's edge over the highway's rumble strip. The beats shook the entire vehicle directly through Marco's forearm and into Erin. she shrieked as her wish arrived, "Cuuuuuuuuuummmmmmmmmmmm". Her pussy twitched violently. Then, pulsed again, harder this time, sending shockwaves through her body as her breath caught in her throat.

Her body detonated. Her internal engine redlined. Every mental gauge shattered as smoke clouded her thoughts. Marco was trying to wring every last ounce of tension from her trembling form. She stomped her feet, kicked wildly, her muscles betraying her attempts to thrust forward. The seat belt kept her locked in place, heightening her surrender. "Fuuuccckkk," she gasped, her voice cracking as her pussy lips fluttered around his fingers, clenching in desperate waves of release.

Her legs collapsed, wrapping around Marco's hand as if they could hold him there forever. She was not letting go.

"Fuuuuuuuuuck," she cried out again, her voice raw, as her body continued to shudder uncontrollably, "I can't stop". Her breasts pressed against her arms, flush from the body's convulsions. The crashing waves of her orgasm tore through her, each surge a violent release of pent-up energy that reverberated out into the world through her trembling, gasping body. Her peaks swelled, collided, and tumbled, leaving her floating in their wake - spent, satisfied, and completely consumed by the man who had driven her there.

Erin lingered on the edge of that blissful apex, her body pulsing with aftershocks as they rippled through her. The engine's growl softened, and she felt Marco ease off the accelerator, as if the car itself were reluctantly surrendering to Marco's suggestion. The powerful hum quieted, though Erin's legs continued to tremble, her breath came in short wheezing gasps as her body downshifted, mirroring the machine beneath them.

The smooth pavement of a long, arched exit ramp greeted them, the gentle embankment soothed her back into reality. The engine groaned in protest, much like her body, wanting just a little more time to play on the open road. But Erin welcomed the pause, giving her the chance to reassemble the pieces of herself that had momentarily scattered.

Her mind, once clouded by adrenaline and desire, slowly cleared as the familiar details of the world around her began to take shape again. Yet, beneath that reconnection to reality, she knew something profound had shifted. The world finally started to catch back up with them. But she knew they could outrun it whenever they wanted. Escape on demand.

Marco's hand returned to the console between them, but continued to loosely intertwine his fingers with Erin's, a tether that kept the intimacy alive. The car glided effortlessly along the exit ramp, smooth and unhurried, giving them time to bask in the silence.

Recognizing the extended length of the ramp, Erin exhaled a breathy laugh, realizing that she'd just had an orgasm in front of her ultimate crush. She broke the spell by saying, "This doesn't feel like an exit".

Marco's lips curled into a knowing smile; his eyes soft yet full of promise. "No," he murmured, his voice carrying the weight of something deeper. "It doesn't... this feelz like zee beginning.

The fire has only just begun to burn. Dare to go deeper? Subscribe for updates to Morgan's private collection at www.TheKnightOfRomance.com.

Stranger Moments

Dark, smooth, and dangerously irresistible, you will be hard pressed to find a story as full bodied as this one. The first sip brims with defiance, a woman reclaiming her night with quiet confidence. But beneath the surface, something illicit stirs, a slow-burning heat that deepens with each stolen glance and each forbidden touch. As the night unfolds, velvety layers of tension fade into lingering seductiveness, making the evening utterly unforgettable - like a pleasure too intoxicating to resist.

Suggested Pairings

Wine: Châteauneuf-du-Pape

Cocktail: Black Velvet

Coffee: Midnight Mocha Seduction

Zero Proof: Dark Cherry & Vanilla Sparkler

Relish!
Morgan Knight

The libations linger long after the last page their recipes can be found at www.*TheKnightOfRomance*.com

"He's not coming", Michele said as she glanced at her watch, a reluctant acceptance was settling in. Here she was, standing at the movie theater entrance, dressed to kill in her flirty mini skirt, a daring low-cut top with an exposed back, and her signature "come fuck me" pumps. Yet, in Chad's absence, the ensemble felt less like a celebration of her confidence and more like a spotlight on her vulnerability. "Ugh, I look like a woman who gets stood up", she thought.

With a mix of hope and irritation, she checked her phone again, expecting at least a missed call or a text. "If he wanted to cancel, he'd say something," she reasoned. Whether it was because he was sick, caught up in an emergency, or simply lost interest, a little communication was the least he could do. But there was nothing. No missed calls. No messages. Just silence.

She had met Chad at the gym, and if you asked her, she'd confess, "Not gonna lie, I was hooked by his physique." Nearly sculpted. He would train in the area of the gym dedicated to professional bodybuilders, feeding on their energy, but refrained from entering their world of injections and meaty muscle compositions. The result was a vigorous body possessing the appeal of a natural warrior from yesteryear. Michele would often gush, "He's got that angled muscle thing along his abs. I don't know what that is, but DAMN!"

While riding the elliptical, she'd watch his muscles run through their sequencing, resembling a machine. Every movement was mechanically mesmerizing. Words like *horsepower* and *cylinder heads* came to mind for her. She'd always considered herself to have the same amorous drive that men have, so when he stepped onto the cool-down mat, Michele always imagined herself lying under him as those intense arms lowered himself onto her.

Their connection was as straightforward as it was electric. One evening, Michele boiled up enough steam in her kettle of courage and approached him. A banter sparked between them, and after a playful razzing about her name possessing only one "L", she found herself enjoying a recovery meal with him. And a bit later, she found herself in his bed.

From the start, he was intense. Fiery. Insatiable. His stamina? Seemingly endless. Together, they fed the raw, animalistic energy crackling between them, each movement a collision of need and desire. Years of cardio and yoga had sculpted her body, training the delicate muscles that could now grip him with delicate precision. The mere thought of him pulsing deep within her sent waves of bliss coursing through her. Yet, it was not just the physical connection, it was the way he *wanted* her, the unfiltered hunger in his touch. That longing, that urgency, only fueled her own, setting every nerve alight with anticipation and pleasure.

At times, he would tease her mercilessly, pulling back just enough to hover at her entrance, until she begged him to take her. Her body would arch towards him with her arms and legs locking around him as tightly as her hunger for him. She knew he was taking her to new points of no return, because in their hazy moments, she heard herself release uncontrollable and breathless squeals - an unfamiliar, thrilling sound - and ones that she'd never made before. Her tones filled the space between them, as he did this again...and again.

Michele relished the specialness she felt when watching his own animalistic nature consume him, overtaking him with an athletically rapid pace. Then, with a final, shuddering groan, he would surrender - thrusting deep. His release would spill into her as she gasped, trembling beneath him. Spent and breathless, he would collapse against her, his weight pressing into her bare skin, the heat of their bodies mingling in the aftermath.

He loved to brag about his prowess in the bedroom, and she, ever independent, dismissed her girlfriends' warnings about his reputation as a serial user of women. With a defiant smirk, she would counter, "He can use me any way that he wants."

Deep down, though, she wasn't sure where things were headed. Always priding herself on her independence and determination, chasing exactly what she wanted without letting anything stand in her way, Michele embraced her strong sexual nature as a testament to her power. *Truth is the nectar that a powerful woman feeds upon*, she reminded herself. And yet, amidst that confidence, a subtle vulnerability tugged at her heart, a truth she could not ignore. Could Chad, and maybe her own ego, get in the way of fully becoming that independent woman? No matter what the future held, one fact remained indisputable: the sex was absolutely incredible.

That truth started to come to life as over the past week, Michele had noticed his gym visits growing increasingly sporadic. He brushed it off with a nonchalant smile, insisting he never stuck with anything for too long and always sought out new thrills. In hindsight, Michele's ego had realized that his restless philosophy was not just for workouts, but applied to people, too.

Now, standing at the theater ticket window on a buzzing Saturday night, she watched the line thin out as couples streamed inside for the popular movie screening. With each ticket sold, his absence became even more palpable, a silent, cutting confirmation. Chad was a no-show.

~ ~

Five minutes remained before the movie started, and Michele felt the weight of a looming decision. Should she head home to nurse her bruised ego? Maybe get drunk? Call a friend and get drunk? Or... she could just step inside...watch the movie on her own. She wasn't new to flying solo. Hell, she'd dined alone in restaurants - enjoying her own company or maybe a book. Tonight, she had only a large fashion magazine that she'd previously purchased, but that hardly mattered.

She couldn't shake the irony: why did the thought of watching a movie alone in a dark theater seem to sting? For goodness' sake, she was a grown woman. She had specifically chosen this movie because she genuinely wanted to see it. She looked forward to it, and the sex that would inevitably follow. Sure, she could always wait for it to appear on Netflix, Prime, or even DVD. She could then return home and take care of that nagging sexual itch with "Dr. Love," the name she'd prescribed to her one and only toy.

As the last couple entered, the thought of murdering Chad with her bare hands swirled around her mind for a moment before she quickly released the emotion. This was just ego. Deep down, she knew she was bigger than his game. He was a brief interlude, maybe even a distraction, and she was not about to let him ruin her night, nor take her independence. Powerful women don't allow small fries to stand in their way.

With renewed resolve, she approached the ticket window, her venturesome spirit shining through. Locking eyes with the bored teenager behind the counter, she articulated those words which endorsed her personal power, "One, please."

The disenchanted young man behind the ticket booth sighed and pointed to the computer screen displaying the theater layout. "We only have these seats free. Where would you like to sit?" he asked, his tone as indifferent as his expression.

Michele would have preferred the back - like when she was sixteen, hanging out with girlfriends at the theatre. Back then, you could sit anywhere. No assigned seating. Places are always more fun in the back. The back of a school bus, the back of the bar, the back of the class. It's where those who goof-off reside. Those who are more fun. The movie theatre was no different. Plus, you can see the whole screen from the back. This new system of choosing your own seat was a little annoying.

Yet, nothing irked her more than the dismissive air of the teenage ticket agent. She couldn't help but wonder if today's youth had truly lost their knack for genuine courtesy. Knowing every generation looks down on the one behind them, she mused, "Were we that awful?". Finally, the attendant offered in his monotone voice, "How about in the middle of this row?" With few other appealing options, Michele relented, letting go of her nostalgic ideal as she accepted the suggested seat.

~ ~

The theater was already bathed in a low, ambient glow. Another dismissive teen with a tiny flashlight escorted her to her row. Michele had to request pardons from several people as she meandered the stream of legs, popcorn boxes, and candy wrappers. In her mind, she could almost hear the murmurs of judgment from those around her, as they sighed through the inconvenience. She continued whispering apologies and polite *"excuse me"'s* until she reached her seat.

Settling in, Michele surveyed her neighbors. To her right, a girl was cozily nestled against her boyfriend, her wavy blonde hair softly resting on his shoulder. The couple had fashioned a makeshift wall out of popcorn boxes and placed it between the girl's seat and Michele's. A privacy fence, perhaps?

On her opposing side sat a strikingly handsome gentleman wearing a crisp green shirt, dark pants, and resting in his lap was a neatly folded sport coat containing a paisley pocket handkerchief. Michele thought he could easily play a young George Clooney in a documentary about the famous actor. In a fleeting daydream, she mentally titled the documentary, *Mr. Handsome.*

Trying not to make either of her neighbors uncomfortable, she eased into her seat and discreetly adjusted her skirt. *There isn't too much to adjust,* she mused, aware of how it barely covered her hips. She forgave herself for her appearance by remembering that the outfit had not been entirely her choice. Chad had requested that she wear something with "easy access" so that he could take advantage of her during the show. At the time, the thought thrilled her but now left her questioning if she just looked more vulgar. She draped the fashion magazine across her knees hoping to cloak at least some of her exposed skin. Fortunately, with the theater's dim lighting and the bright previews playing she could barely even make out the magazine when she looked down.

For a brief moment, Michele entertained the idea of firing off a scathing text to Chad, unloading all her frustrations about his shallow, self-centered nature and the awkward position he'd forced her into. Again, ego surfacing. And, as quickly as the thought arose, she dismissed it with a resigned, "What's the point?" The opening scene began, and her attention fully shifted to the screen.

Michele knew this flick would captivate her. Action, romance, poetic sex, all rolled into one. Two lovers faced the world together with no apparent chance of escaping the numerous challenging situations. She was hyped-up with anticipation, when - unexpectedly, Michele felt something brush against her ankle. Probably a candy wrapper, she assumed, then adjusted and ignored the impression. Until...the sensation persisted. She squinted into the darkness and realized that the man beside her had nudged her bare ankle with his shoe. He appeared absorbed in the movie, oblivious, or perhaps unconcerned, about the physical contact. With a careful movement, she pulled her foot away, deciding to let the moment pass.

On her opposing side, the girlfriend was engrossed in a slow, but alluring, make out session with her boyfriend. With their intimate dance of soft lips, wet tongues, and lingering kisses, Michele could not help but relish in being their peripheral voyeur. Coupled with the steamy romance unfolding on screen, her own hormones were beginning to simmer.

Michele returned her attention to the projected story on the screen. A moment or two passed when she noticed a faint pressure register against her calf, so subtle that she nearly dismissed it as her imagination. Glancing down, she saw that *Mr. Handsome* had shifted slightly, his leg now gently pressing against hers. The rough texture of his pants contrasted deliciously with the smoothness of her bare skin, creating a rather sensual sensation.

Hmm, she mused, *what to do?* By all social conventions, she had every right to deliver a swift kick or drive her sharp heel into his foot. He would have gotten the message. But as she weighed her options, she noticed herself enjoying the sensation. This was not at all unpleasant, quite the opposite really. Soothing. Maybe even intriguing. So much so that when his fingers lightly grazed her lower thigh, she didn't startle. The subtle touch did not feel abrupt or out of place. Instead, it added to the quiet pulse of heat simmering beneath her skin.

Had her silence given him unspoken permission? What exactly was unfolding here? Some erotic exploration by two strangers in a large, darkened theater full of people? She certainly wasn't in any danger, and somehow, she knew that if she signaled for him to stop, he would do so immediately. Another thought flickered through her mind, *Could anyone else see what he was doing to her?* The idea of an openly secret exchange sent a delicious shiver down her spine.

His contact was featherlight, barely more than a whisper against her skin, like the brush of the finest velvet. A quiet tremor rippled through Michele, though outwardly, she remained composed, her eyes fixed on the screen. By all social measures, she was just another audience member, immersed in the film, absorbing the soundtrack. But beneath that facade, she was slipping into a parallel universe, one ruled by pure physical sensation.

His fingertips traced slow, deliberate paths along her thigh, igniting a restless heat beneath her skin. She wondered if he knew just how deeply he was affecting her. *He must*, she thought, because each time she tried to predict his movements, his touch deepened. Shudders rolled through her, as he pushed the boundaries with unhurried confidence. His hand inched higher, slipping beneath the thin edge of her skirt. Anticipation coiled inside Michele like a live wire.

And then... he stopped.

Michele froze, caught in the breathless stillness of the moment. Was he hesitating? Second-guessing? Her mind looped through a rapid cycle of indignation, frustration, and sheer aching excitement. *Don't stop now.* The moment was too charged, too irresistible to let slip away.

Michele exhaled a slow, deliberate sigh, a perceptible implication that stamped his permission slip to continue. Actually, it was more of a request. Maybe even a demand. His hand resumed the steady ascent, fingertips tracing the sensitive skin of her inner thigh, edging closer to the heat pooling between her legs. Her pussy, already wet, tantalizingly close to his reach.

With an almost reverent touch, he slipped aside the thin lace of her thong. She swore she heard a sharp inhale, perhaps a quiet gasp of appreciation at how neatly groomed she was. His fingers traced the delicate contours of her lips, mapping the wetness that testified to her arousal.

Michele sat perfectly still, as if spellbound. The soft press of his middle finger gently parted her with effortless ease, sinking inside, while his thumb began a slow, knowing rhythm against her clit. She melted into the sensation, her body responding instinctively, her wetness guiding him.

For a moment, he withdrew, and she watched in a dazed fascination as he brought his fingers to his lips, tasting her wetness with an expression of pure indulgence. The sheer audacity of it sent a jolt of excitement through her, a sharp pulse of pleasure and anticipation. Without thinking, she shifted, her hand inadvertently landing in his lap.

Michele's breath caught in her throat. He was bare. Hard. Waiting. Had he also been touching himself with his other hand, as he explored her? The thought sent another wave of heat surging through her.

He had draped his sport coat over his lap, a makeshift shield against prying eyes. But beneath it, the heat between them burned unchecked. As his fingers found their way back to her, Michele reached for him in turn, wrapping her hand around the solid weight of his arousal. His touch resumed its slow, deliberate dance over her wetness, teasing, exploring.

She arched her head back, outwardly giving the impression of an audience member shifting from a stiff neck, but in reality, she was trying to stretch the mounting tension from her spine. The kind of tension that only he could now release. Her grip tightened, relishing the firmness of him, his warmth pulsing in her palm.

Her eyes remained locked on the screen, unable to turn and meet his gaze. Ordinarily, she would have been lost in moans by now, surrendering to pleasure, but here, she had to remain silent, composed, pretending to be absorbed in the film even as desire consumed her. The secrecy only heightened the thrill. This was theirs alone, a wicked, unspeakable indulgence unfolding in the shadows, unseen yet electrifyingly real.

Maintaining the illusion of composure while his fingers incited chaos beneath the surface was nearly impossible. He pushed deeper inside her, his movements deliberate, unrelenting. Swallowing her moans was an exercise in restraint, a battle she was quickly losing. If he kept this up, Michele knew, without question, that she would unravel right here, in the middle of the theater. In public. And as soon as that thought crossed her mind, the impulse arrived.

Her free hand pressed over his, anchoring him inside her as the first wave crashed through her. In her other hand, she felt him pulsing, his arousal now matching her own. A shudder rippled through Michele. To an outside observer, it could have passed as a chill, an involuntary tremor. But inside, she was coming undone. Another contraction gripped her, then another, each one rolling through her in deep, breath-stealing pulses. Her pussy lips clenched around his fingers, holding him captive as her body took over, claiming him in silent, unbridled pleasure.

In that same moment, she felt him release, hot and slick against her fingers. He pulsed in her grasp, mirroring the rhythm of her own trembling depths. His thumb found her clit, delivering another jolt, sending another contraction tearing through her. Her leg quivered, her grip on the seat tightened. She squeezed him in return, feeling his throbs, absorbing his energy into the raw, electric pulse of her own climax.

The intensity blurred the edges of reality. Dizzy with pleasure, she closed her eyes, surrendering to the moment, letting the aftershocks consume her as the waves slowed their roll through her. Inevitably, they began to dissipate and evolved into simple comforts of touch, leaving them in a still, weightless silence.

Neither moved, neither spoke. Their eyes remained fixed on the screen, but their hands told a different story. Their fingers remained entwined in the massaging aftermath of something unspoken, something electric. No one around them had the slightest idea of what had just passed between them. This belonged to them alone, a secret moment suspended in time.

Slowly, his hand withdrew, but not before one final act of reverence. He brought his fingers, slick with Michele's essence, to his lips once more, savoring her with the same quiet appreciation as before. Michele watched, enthralled. Then, with an effortless elegance, he reached into his sport coat pocket, retrieving the neatly folded paisley handkerchief and offered it to her.

Michele met his gaze and would eventually accept the offer. But, not before sharing a wordless echo of gratitude and connection by lifting a single delicate fingertip to her lips and tasting him in return.

This is merely the beginning. Morgan has more to share, if you're brave enough to ask at www.*TheKnightOfRomance*.com.

Horsin' Around

This story pours like a bold, untamed Malbec - dark, smoky, and laced with danger. It opens with deep blackberry and earthy richness, much like Kayla's quiet strength and steady resolve. But just beneath, there's a rebellious edge - ripe plum and spice, mirroring the outlaw's wild, unbreakable spirit. Notes of leather and dark cocoa hint at temptation, the kind that lingers on the palate like an unshakable desire. And the finish? Velvety, sultry, and impossible to resist - just like the tension crackling between them, no matter how dangerous it may be.

Suggested Pairings

Wine: Malbec (Mendoza)

Cocktail: Smoky Maple Bourbon Smash

Coffee: Iced Honey Cinnamon Latte

Zero Proof: Smoked Vanilla Root Beer

Immerse Yourself!
Morgan Knight

Every alluring pour from these pages is yours to recreate.
These recipes live at www.*TheKnightOfRomance*.com

"Another horse farm? You've got to be kidding me, Daddy," Kayla protested, folding her arms and glaring up the stairs.

"Fresh air," her father called down, as if that would sweeten the deal.

"It's Iowa, Daddy. There's fresh air everywhere," she shot back, rolling her eyes before pausing. "What is it this time?"

"A horse trailer," he shouted, "and it's a 'Beast'".

Kayla frowned. "Where?"

Silence.

Her irritation bubbled over as she repeated the question, her voice sharper. "Where, Daddy?"

Still no answer.

Her annoyance meter red lined, "Daddy, where the hell is - "

The sound of his boots clomping down the stairs interrupted her. Her father emerged, folding up the cuffs of his plaid shirt as he took a seat on the bottom step. With a heavy sigh, he looked her straight in the eye and said, "McKintrick's."

Her laugh came automatically, as if it had to be a joke. But the humor drained from her face when she saw that he was serious.

"No. No, no, no. Daddy, you cannot be serious!"

He didn't flinch. Calm and unwavering, he delivered the verdict. "Just go. Pick up the trailer. It's parked out front. You won't have to talk to anyone."

Kayla huffed, but her father wasn't budging. As if to end the conversation, he mused, "Take the F450. That'll pull my new 'Beast'."

She narrowed her eyes at him, but when his expression didn't waver, she knew she'd lost this battle.

Kayla's fiery gaze locked onto her father's steady eyes, but her intensity did nothing to shake him. If anything, he seemed mildly amused, like he'd seen this storm a hundred times before and knew exactly how it would end. Her frustration, once blazing, would eventually fizzle under the weight of his calm resolve, like a match drowned in water. With a huff, she spun on her heel, snatched the keys from the rack, and threw open the screen door. As she stomped down the porch steps, the heat of her fit was already beginning to cool into mild frustration, fading like distant thunder after a passing storm.

~ ~

Kayla favored the F450, seeing a kindred spirit in the truck. To the untrained eye, this was just another pickup. But the 450 held a secret. Under the hood lurked a force. A force that could pull continents into an ocean. Likewise, to the unknowing eye, Kayla was just another member of her community. But she too held a secret. Under her own hood lurked a force. A force that had yet to find an outlet, or anyone who could put it in gear.

So, the 450 remained her favorite. Sure, there were other haulers she could choose, and most women would not dream of handling the rigs Kayla was licensed to drive. Big machines intimidate most folks. But her father, a self-made man and former hell-raiser, would not settle for raising a dependent daughter. And so, he taught her. Decades ago, when he first arrived in their conservative community, the locals required years to adjust to his eccentric ways. In the end though, no one could deny his knack for getting the tough things done, which eventually won them over.

Persistence was his secret weapon. Though Kayla would never admit it aloud, she admired that about him. His relentless drive seeped into her like rain soaking the soil, silent but nourishing. When the storms of life hit hard with drenching downpours, gusty winds, and the crackle of threatening lightning, other men surrendered, waiting for clearer skies. Usually, these men were then stuck in the mud. But not her father. He trudged on, even as the mud swallowed his knees. One step at a time. One grueling, filthy struggle after another. Until, eventually, he would reach his goal, whatever that might be.

Kayla had absorbed those lessons without even realizing it. She had not earned her engineering degree or rig licenses through brilliance or shortcuts. Nope. She got them through persistence - one grueling class, one tough, muddy exam at a time, following her father's demonstration.

Kayla's fury had simmered into a low boil as she climbed into the cab of the 450. The heavy rumble of the diesel greeted her as she cranked it to life. But that greeting did little to soften her mood. "Fuckin' man's world," she churned, gripping the steering wheel. Everything around her screamed *man's stuff*: trucks, trailers, horses. Well, she did like the horses, the dogs too. But the shovels, rakes, whips, and dirt-streaked chores? All *man's stuff*. "We could use some girl stuff around here," she grumbled under her breath.

But Kayla was not being fully honest with herself. In truth, she thrived on the masculine energy surrounding her. She actually loved the grit, the noise, and the power. She felt alive around it. What really had her stomping out of the house was not the trucks or the trailers, nor the shovels or the rakes, not even the dirt. It was the name - *McKintrick*.

That family had always held a strange place in her life, especially their son. They had grown up together with Kayla graduating a year behind him. Though she could not point to specific examples that highlighted a rebellious nature, his reputation in high school was not *James Dean*, but maybe more *Jesse James*. Older generations referred to him as "a rascal", and most folks said he was like Forrest Gump's box of chocolates, "You never know what you're gonna get with McKintrick". For Kayla, that had always translated to just one word: *unstable*. And even though she didn't really know him, the very idea of him still sent jitters down her spine.

She knew driving would soothe her nerves though. As she pulled away from the gravel driveway and onto the open road, the steady hum of the 450's diesel washed over her like a familiar lullaby. She gripped the wheel a little tighter, letting the machine's rhythmic vibrations soothe her tension.

"I do like the power of this thing," she murmured. What she really meant was that the machine felt alive beneath her. The slow, steady acceleration matched her mood perfectly, building momentum with purpose. The low rumble of the engine pulsed through her seat, a sensation that settled deep within her, making her smile.

More than once, she'd considered pulling over on some deserted dirt road. Maybe lay her seat back and rev the engine for ten minutes or so, soaking in those teasing vibrations. The rhythmic strokes of the valve licks and rocker arms could echo through her seat until they turned a bad afternoon into a pretty damn good day.

But this being Iowa, fantasies had their limits. Inevitably, some well-meaning local farmer and his wife would come trundling down the dirt road and spot her parked truck. They'd assume the worst. Then rap their knuckles on her fogged-up windows while shouting a muffled "You okay?" That's where the fantasy always collapsed. Because how do you explain to someone that you were not using a truck engine to masturbate?

Still, the truth was that she spent nearly her entire life under a host of male influences. She was drawn to this lifestyle, to the ruggedness of the farm community where men made decisions based on hard facts, brute force, and simple, practical logic. Her femininity craved the swirl of these masculine energies, and Kayla often wondered why.

Most women in the community quietly fell in line, slipping into their traditional roles with minimal complaint or, maybe while muttering quiet qualms between one another. Kayla had always noticed how their passive acceptance aged them more rapidly, the weight of their silence pressing down like the sun baking the fields. Not Kayla. She was not built for quiet compliance. She would not follow in these women's footsteps. No. She spoke up. She'd been raised to. But she did so when situations called for it, not when personal insecurities arose. Not to stand out. Not to demonstrate her individuality.

She knew that a modern feminist would not be awarded much respect in her community. Most likely, they would attribute any man's dismissiveness to the man being "sexist". Kalya understood that this was not at all true. These men were honest and responsible, which meant they would call out *anyone* who was being irrational, regardless of gender. More often than not, the men in her community openly criticized other men for being a bonehead, or dim witted, or irrational, or an idiot, or insecure, or soft, or dense. If someone at a community meeting was being a brainless, weak-minded moron, the reason was not because of whatever secrets they had tucked between the pockets of their Levi's. The reason was because they were a brainless, weak-minded moron. Gender was irrelevant.

Being as outspoken as her father, attacks were certain to point themselves in Kayla's direction from time to time. But she never attributed any of the criticisms as an affront to her womanhood. And for that, the men in the community respected her.

Could the men be more polite? Sure. Could they use some manners? Absolutely. Were they uneducated? Yep, most of them, anyway. But they did live their lives with purpose, and one that they chose. Kayla may not have always agreed with their *how*, but she always tipped her hat to their *why*.

Being besieged by these masculine vibes still delighted her. But she could never figure out why. Once she came across a magazine article that shed a little light on the phenomenon. A researcher at Rutgers, Dr. Helen Fischer, suggested why we like who we like. Essentially, why is it that we fall in love with person A over person B, or person C. The reason? Hormones. No, not just feeling turned on by somebody. But the biological makeup of your own hormones.

It's the three bears, really. Person A might have too much dopamine. Person B might not have enough estrogen. But person C's level of serotonin is juuuuuusssssstttt right. There's a fourth hormone that figures into our biological cocktail. Testosterone. The sex hormone. When Kayla read this, she wondered if maybe the cosmic bartender spiked her being with a double shot of that lustful firewater.

And yet, despite being surrounded by all that masculine blaze, Kayla was undeniably feminine. Calendar girl legs, an hour-glass figure, and breasts so enviable that her white tank tops would celebrate being chosen for an outfit the way "Price Is Right" contestants celebrated winning the showcase showdown. She had the body of a pin-up girl, and the mindset of a farmhand. Somewhere in that blend of curves and grit, she was beginning to successfully carve out her own place in the world.

But inside, she burned. The constant hunger gnawed at her, maddening and insatiable. Kayla understood men in a way most women did not because when it came to desire, she believed she was just like them. Remember? Testosterone. "Sometimes", she often thought, "you just need to be fucked". But finding a partner who could meet her intensity, who could match her unpredictableness - sometimes tender and slow, other times raw and wild - felt almost impossible. That duality she held unsettled her, a side of herself she feared others would judge harshly if they knew the truth.

The problem wasn't her, but the community. Conservative. Traditional values. And, in small communities, reputation is everything. Small towns are true democracies, where give and take have been an effective survival strategy since humans moved in tribes. That's what a small town is, a tribe. History is flooded with individuals who were blacklisted for disobeying this natural decree.

Small communities function like living organisms. Balance and cooperation are mechanisms for the tribe's survival, and indulgent self-interest is viewed as a threat. Anyone who pushes those limits, anyone who indulges too much, threatens to harm the tribe. So, they're usually ostracized, to prevent weakening the whole. Which is why, at the end of the day, Kayla felt lonely regarding this facet of her character. She wondered if her father knew her well enough to understand. Obviously, discussing how randy you often feel was not something most people brought up at the dinner table.

As the 450 hummed beneath her, teasing her through the vibrations of the seat, Kayla let the rolling hills of Iowa lull her into reflection. Flyover folks think Iowa is flat. No. Kansas is flat, as is Eastern Colorado. Iowa?

Hilly. Here, the hills undulated gently, the kind of ride that felt like a slow, soothing kiddie roller coaster. The road's rhythm encouraged her thoughts to wander, and just as all wandering thoughts do, they landed on the reason for her uneasiness, on what she was mentally avoiding, her destination - McKintrick's.

Her mind slipped back to high school like a tape rewinding itself. The echo of a locker slamming. Two girls giggling over one's boyfriend. *"Oh my God, he's so..."* more giggles. And there, like a shadow on the edge of memory - McKintrick. The town's outlier. The kid that no one trusted but everyone secretly watched. He was not the charming rebel, not the brooding type who left girls swooning. No, he was something wilder, more unpredictable. Like I said, the older folks called him "a rascal," but to Kayla, he'd always been like a coiled spring, you never knew when or how he'd snap.

He did not strut through the halls as a king or a misfit. He was simply...untouchable. Not quite a delinquent, but not someone you wanted to test, either. Rumors swirled about him constantly, whispered tales of fights, pranks, and mysterious misdeeds, but there was never any evidence to socially convict him. Regardless, Kayla had no doubt that McKintrick's high school rap sheet included more than a few stunts that evaded the principal's office and the police. For reasons she did not fully understand, thinking about him still gave her the jitters.

That's when she rounded the hilltop mound and spotted the rusted mailbox. The faded letters had long since abandoned the steel frame, leaving it to read: *M Kintri k.* The sight tugged at her memory, but she brushed it off as she crept the 450 into the pea gravel driveway, her eyes scanning the property through the windshield.

The residence resembled something from a ghost story. The barn leaned slightly, its wood weathered and grayed, while patches of overgrown grass and forgotten machinery dotted the landscape like abandoned relics. The place was quiet, uncomfortably quiet, and Kayla could not help but grit her teeth. "So, this is where the famous McKintrick lives, huh?" she muttered.

The driveway looped around a small roundabout. Kayla shut down the engine, letting the sudden silence swallow her. She caught a fleeting glimpse of herself in the rearview mirror, her fingers instinctively smoothing a stray strand of hair. As her boots met the earth, a quiet revelation brushed against her thoughts. *Did I just check myself?* The question unfurled like a whisper in the wind. She blinked, shook her head, and let it drift away.

Yet even as the thought faded, her gaze had already swept downward, skimming the length of her shorts - a reflexive move she knew too well. The 450 stirred more than just her frustration on drives; but awoke something unspoken, something she was not ready to name. And now, standing on the edge of McKintrick's territory, she felt the sudden need to ensure her Daisy Dukes had not betrayed her. The last thing she wanted was for McKintrick to find her looking like she had just stepped out of a daydream she should not have been having.

A hush blanketed McKintrick's property, the kind of stillness that made Kayla wonder if the place had been abandoned. "It's NOT 'right out front,' Daddy!" she muttered under her breath. In fact, the trailer wasn't anywhere in sight. Maybe her father had purchased the horse trailer from another farm, maybe an auction that he'd forgotten about. As she scanned the yard, her frustration built. The warm Iowa breeze slipped through her white tank top, cooling her sun-kissed breasts as she squinted toward the barn.

Then, a voice - distant, but strong - called out, "It's 'round back."

She jumped, spinning around. *Where had that come from?* She scanned the landscape, her eyes darting between shadows and sunlit patches of overgrown grass. Then, she heard it again - a low, amused laugh, guiding her gaze upward.

There, in the second-story loft of the barn he stood - McKintrick. The "rascal" himself. The young man she'd been conditioned to avoid, thanks to years of high school gossip and small-town whispers. Her heart stuttered as she tried to reconcile her expectations with what she was now seeing. *That's not to be feared,* she thought. *That's...* "Normal" was an attempt at a word she'd been aiming for, but as he turned to toss a bale of hay to the back of the loft, she realized her mistake. *"Normal"* did not fit, either. The most appropriate word was *"ripped"*.

Most farming men carried beer guts or at least a hint of one, but not McKintrick. His body was carved, a testament to long hours of physical work. His tanned lats flared like wings, his broad shoulders practically shouting *deltoids*, while his arms - the biceps, the triceps, and forearms moved in perfect synchronization. They were not just muscles; they were a display of raw power and control, rippling like waves across a still lake after a drop of rain.

Kayla swallowed hard. *That's not what they told me to expect.*

Kayla reminded herself of what she'd heard growing up: "Oh, right. Not James Dean, but more Jesse James." *With McKintrick, you never knew what you were gonna get.* But as she watched him now, a thought crept in. *Was his reputation for being unstable earned, or was it just another misunderstanding, like the way the town had misunderstood her father's eccentric ways in his early days?*

Shaking off the thought, she cupped her hands and called up to the loft, "What?"

"The trailer," he huffed, wiping sweat from his brow. "It's 'round back." He threw one last hay bale into the pile, then glanced down at the ground from the second story. Then, he jumped.

Kayla's eyes widened as she watched him plunge straight into the center of a haystack, the kind of bold move that had her thinking, *Who does that?* Maybe the rumors were not entirely off the mark.

McKintrick emerged from the hay, shaking loose the golden strands that clung to him. He strode toward her, his boots sinking slightly into the mud on each step, the afternoon sun catching on the sweat-slicked planes of his tanned skin. His shirtless overalls clung to him, worn like a second skin.

"It's stuck in the mud, though," he said, pausing mid-step to rub his nose, the dust from the hay teased his senses. With an easy motion, he tugged off his leather gloves, revealing hands rough with calluses yet deliberate in their movements - strong, but tempered with control. He extended one toward her, his grip steady, his voice simple and unhurried.

"Hi. I'm McKintrick."

"I know," Kayla huffed, offering a small, shy grin.

His brow furrowed slightly, and she realized with a pang of disappointment, that he had not remembered her from high school. Her ego deflated, shrinking in the space between them. In less than thirty seconds, she'd seen him shift from a reckless barn jumper to a polite gentleman, then to someone who did not seem to give her a second thought. *They were right,* she thought bitterly. *With McKintrick, you never know what you're gonna get.*

"You're here for the trailer, right?" McKintrick confirmed, leading her around the back of the barn. As he passed, Kayla noticed the way his gaze momentarily lingered on her cleavage, just a beat too long to be accidental. Her lips parted slightly, but she did not call him out on it. Instead, she fell in step behind him. "Yes," she answered, her voice calm, masking the flutter in her chest.

"Well, like I said, it's stuck in the mud," he said with a casual huff, trudging ahead without concern for the mess beneath his boots. Kayla sighed, hopping between patches of dry ground to avoid the worst of the sludge. "How the hell," she asked mid-hop, "do we get it out?"

"That's gonna be quite the workout," McKintrick replied with a smirk.

Kayla nearly smiled. "A workout," she thought, "That is exactly what I need." She was being serious. Between the teasing vibrations of the drive and the view of McKintrick's built, sweat-slicked body, she felt like a fuse waiting to ignite. The lingering tension from his unpredictable reputation only fueled her further. A task like pushing a trailer through the mud? That was the perfect way to burn off the restless energy humming inside her.

Her gaze remained projected onto the ground as she carefully navigated the puddles and clogs of mud, until her attention was stolen by something towering ahead. Kayla stopped and looked upward - stunned. She was standing at the feet of an absolutely phenomenal home, still under construction. *Was this a renovation?* From the ground up, the foundation incorporated the features of an exquisite barn, complete with luxurious horse paddocks. But then, the structure expanded into exquisite living quarters above. Columns of smooth river stone wrapped themselves around heavy support beams while decks jutted out from each level, offering sweeping views of the 80 rolling acres beyond. The upper floors offered unique elegance by combining warm wood and glass, incorporating a stone fireplace in nearly every major room. The structure embraced a distinctive signature where rustic appeal meets modern touches which gave the home a feeling like something from a luxury magazine.

Her breath caught as she absorbed the structure's details. This was not a renovation. This was a masterpiece, built from the ground up. *McKintrick had done this?* As she stood there, surrounded by the quiet hum of prairie winds and the scent of earth, Kayla realized she was not just impressed, she was intrigued. Kayla gasped, unable to help herself. The sheer scale and beauty of the place took her by surprise. McKintrick heard her and stopped mid-step, turning to face the creation of wood and stone behind him. He didn't puff up with pride or act impressed by her reaction. Instead, he shrugged casually and said, "Yeah. My side project."

Kayla blinked, still struggling to process what she was seeing. "Side project?" she whispered, almost in disbelief. This was not a shed or a simple barn conversion, this was architectural art.

McKintrick smirked, shoving his hands into his pockets as if this were no big deal. "You know how this town is," he said. "Gotta put your pent-up energy somewhere, right?" His gaze held a weight to it, and if he was talking about the kind of energy that Kayla thought he was talking about, then she understood **exactly** what he was talking about. Her heart picked up speed. "Will you show it to me?" she asked, her voice softer than she intended.

He let the moment hang before giving a dismissive, almost teasing, "Ahhhh," as if debating whether or not she'd earned the right. His tone left her guessing, but his lingering gaze told her he wasn't shutting the door on the idea entirely.

Her gaze clung to the house as she slowly walked backward, mesmerized by its beauty and craftsmanship. Every detail, the weathered wood, the towering stone columns, the perfectly placed decks overlooking the prairie, felt deliberate, as if each piece held a story. She barely noticed when a puddle splashed against her ankle, dismissing it with a quick thought: *Not my first pair of muddy boots.*

She continued drifting backward, appreciating the structure like a mesmerizing painting that she couldn't tear her eyes from. For a moment, McKintrick's reputation faded into reason. The talent it must have taken to build something this incredible made her feel unexpectedly proud. She felt like she'd discovered buried treasure right out in the open - something precious that others had overlooked. He wasn't an outlaw, she realized. He was an artist. He was eccentric, sure, but so was her father. *He's like Daddy,* she thought, her realization hitting her all at once just as the hard steel frame of the horse trailer slammed into the back of her calf.

"Whoa!" she yelped, stumbling forward.

"Careful," McKintrick chuckled, his voice smooth and easy.

Kayla steadied herself and looked up at him, her breath catching as her stare evolved into something new, something thoughtful. She needed a second to pull herself back from the unexpected connection she'd just made between her father and McKintrick. Shaking it off, she turned to face the trailer, the rusty "Beast" she had been sent to retrieve.

"What a piece of..." she started, but bit her tongue just in time to avoid insulting him. Instead, she let the thought fade, shifting her focus back to the job at hand.

"Tssst. I know," McKintrick confirmed, rubbing the back of his neck. "Not sure why your old man wanted it."

Kayla narrowed her eyes, skeptical. "Are you sure this is the...?"

"Only one I've got," he interrupted. "Couldn't believe what your father offered me. Thought he was nuts. I'm buying a brand-new one with the money." He shrugged, almost apologetic. "Felt bad taking the deal, but he insisted."

Insisted? Kayla frowned. Her father never would have insisted on something as trivial as a beat-up, mud-logged horse trailer. What was he up to? She glanced at the trailer, the tire base marinating in mud.

"This is gonna take both of us," she said, planting her hands on her hips.

"Agreed." McKintrick cracked his knuckles and nodded. "Do you want push, or pull?"

Kayla slowly made her way to the back of the trailer, testing the firmness of the ground with each step. "I'll push to start. We'll probably have to switch." She glanced around the narrow space. "No room for the tractor, and the 450's not getting into this tight space 'til we can get things rolling a few feet. So, it's just you and me."

McKintrick moved to the front of the trailer and braced himself. Their eyes locked on one another, a silent agreement passing between them, an unspoken oath swearing allegiance to one another in their fight against the Beast. "Ready?" His voice cut through the stillness. "Three... two... one...PUSH...PULL!"

The trailer groaned as both of them strained, their breaths heavy and muscles taut. Their teeth gritted. Their eyes remained locked on one another, silently communicating subtle changes about the other's position, or maybe their footing. Each could then quickly adjust as needed. The echo of their grunts along with some choice swear words bounced off the barn walls, blending into the sound of straining metal.

Kayla's gaze darted toward McKintrick, catching the flex of his arms and back as he pulled with raw strength. His muscles rippled with every movement, and for a moment, she found herself distracted by his sheer power.

Meanwhile, McKintrick's focus wavered just as much. As Kayla leaned forward to push, her tank top stretched over her curves, and her body moved with a rhythm that was hard to ignore. He glanced back, catching a glimpse of her before snapping his attention forward, but the image lingered in his mind like an inspirational aftershock.

Neither of them said anything, but the energy between them had shifted, mixing effort with tension, strength with desire. As the Beast defended himself against their attack, Kayla could not help but think that the workout she'd wanted was quickly turning into something far more intense. *Is this flirting?* she wondered, her breath shaking as she pushed harder against the stubborn weight of the trailer. Every grunt and shared effort between them seemed to be charged with something more than just physical strain.

Her thoughts churned in a whirlwind, struggling to settle on the task at hand. But then, as sudden as a struck match, understanding flared. This was never about the trailer. Her father's concern *was* McKintrick. More than that, his concern was about *Kayla finding McKintrick*. And now, standing knee-deep in the mud, the pieces settled into place, forming a truth she could no longer ignore.

Gritting her teeth, she leaned her shoulder into the trailer, putting her full weight behind the push. The wheels creaked and groaned, but she barely noticed. Instead, her thoughts circled back to how much she and McKintrick actually had in common, far more than she would have ever acknowledged. They were both driven, unwilling to give up until they achieved what they wanted. Both were restless, frustrated with the traditional, rigid nature of their small community. And maybe, just maybe, they were two people who could help each other burn off all that bottled-up energy.

She glanced at McKintrick, watching the way his muscles strained through each lurch forward, the sweat gleaming on his tanned skin. He wasn't just brute strength - there was determination in the set of his jaw, the same persistence her father had drilled into her from a young age.

A strange warmth spread through her chest. Her father had seen something she had not, something she might have missed, if not for this moment. He understood his daughter - maybe even better than she understood herself. In an unspoken way, he was acknowledging those aspects of her being that she kept hidden and helping her to express them in healthy manners. He was silently guiding her, as fathers do.

She would never have considered McKintrick on her own. But now, standing here, mud on her boots and perspiration glistening over her breasts, she realized that her father may not have been the only cook in this matchmaking attempt. Fate may have thrown in some spices. And maybe, just maybe, the two old men had cooked up something special.

Suddenly, the Beast let out a surrendering creak, followed by a faint groan. Both Kayla and McKintrick felt the change - a subtle but unmistakable shift, the tires had given way just enough to inspire hope. The trailer began to budge, the wheels sluggishly breaking free of the mud. This minor shared victory fueled them, igniting a second wind. They dug in, pouring every last ounce of strength into the push-pull rhythm.

Teeth gritted. Breath ragged. The air filled with their huffs and groans as the Beast rolled forward, each inch gained amplified their determination. Mud coated the tires as they continued their slow ascent out of the mire, until finally, with one last shove, the trailer broke free and rolled onto firm ground.

They both collapsed into the tall grass at opposite ends of the trailer, breathless and streaked with mud, but with victory humming between them.

Kayla lay there, catching her breath, listening to the distant whirr of insects and the whisper of prairie winds. Sweat ran down her back. Then, she heard the rustle of footsteps through the tall grass. McKintrick was walking past her, his breathing - heavy. "You should be able to pull your truck around now," he said, glancing briefly over his shoulder before continuing toward the barn.

Kayla started after him, her heart thudding, not just from the exertion but from something deeper. *Is this it? Is this moment slipping through my fingers?* She felt a pang of urgency, a whisper inside her that warned her not to let him walk away. He was not just someone she had worked alongside in the mud. He felt like someone who could see her for who she truly was, without the layers of small-town judgment. Someone who could handle the trollop version of herself that she kept locked away.

Kayla needed to stop him. *Desperate times*, she thought, her lips curving into a mischievous grin.

McKintrick's back was still to her when she reached down, scooping a handful of cool, wet mud in her hand. "THWAP." The sling of mud smacked squarely across his backside, splattering against the worn fabric of his overalls.

He stopped in his tracks, his shoulders tensing before he slowly turned. His eyes found her immediately - the guilty party, sitting in the grass, flirtatiously giggling. Her white tank top was gone, left somewhere behind in the tall grass, and her mud-covered right hand held the proof of her crime.

McKintrick stared for a moment, his gaze taking her in - bare skin glowing under the sun, her laughter bubbling up from somewhere free and untamed. Then his lips curved into a slow, wicked grin, as he moved towards her.

Kayla giggled again, a sound light and carefree, even as her pulse raced. She felt unshackled, untamed, and it didn't matter where this led. The heat of the midday sun warmed her bare skin, and the thick summer air wrapped around her like a smothering embrace. McKintrick's face twisted into something between a snarl and a grin, his eyes dark with intention. Kayla's breath slipped past her lips. Fear and exhilaration swirled together, intoxicating her. *You never know what you're gonna get with McKintrick,* she thought, feeling the delicious uncertainty of him closing the distance.

Step by step, he trudged through the mud, and she mirrored him in reverse, her boots squelching as she backed up, her heart thumping harder with each step. This was a dance - one step forward, one step back. He was the moth, and she was the flame. She didn't care. Her backward retreat ended when she bumped into the large rear tire of an old tractor, her breath catching as she realized she was cornered.

McKintrick reached for her, his tone playful, yet predatory. "Ohhhhh," he drawled, "So that's how you wanna play it". His eyes traveled down her body, slow and deliberate, like a wolf savoring the sight of its prey. Kayla felt herself melt under the weight of his gaze, a mixture of submission and thrill flooding through her. She wanted to surrender to him, to be taken, but she still relished the game.

Without warning his fingers intertwined with her hair then instantly closed, gripping several locks into his fist. She gasped, half in alarm, half in delight. He pulled her head back, exposing her throat to the warmth of the sun and the cool breeze of the air around them. His full lips brushed her skin first, soft and sensual, before they pressed more firmly against her neck. He tasted her slowly, tracing kisses down the sensitive curve where her neck met her shoulder, each touch electrifying.

Her head stayed fixed, held securely by his fist, as her body arched toward him. Kayla felt the sweat from his abs flirting with her nipples, sending uncontrollable shivers through her.

"Yes," she breathed, her voice barely more than a whisper. Her fingers trailed down the front of his overalls, sliding effortlessly beneath the fabric until she found him, warm and hard in her grasp. Her fingers seized him with deliberate and teasing pressure, "That's the way I like to play it," she murmured.

McKintrick exhaled sharply, his breath hot against her neck as she gripped him tighter, applying just the right amount of force to match the tension of his hand in her hair. "What about you?" she asked, her tone a mix of curiosity and seduction. He answered by growing harder in her hands. Words were no longer necessary.

Their movements became instinctual, wordless communication passing between them in touches, gasps, and tension as the game shifted into something neither of them could, or wanted to, control. Kayla arched her back as his lips grazed the delicate curve of her neck, soft and tantalizing. His hands slid to her breasts, rough and warm, gently cupping her through the thin layer of mud and sweat that clung to her skin. The earth smearing across her curves felt primal, grounding her in the moment. She intertwined her fingers with his, guiding him, silently teaching him where and when to grip her harder or softer. Every move he made sparked a response, and for every touch, she answered back, building a rhythm that was theirs alone.

When he climbed onto the tractor's rear tire and reached for her, she recognized this for what it was: a move. She grinned inwardly and countered, stepping onto the seat with ease. He followed, closing the distance between. His hands cradled her face, rough palms tender against her cheeks, and then he kissed her - deep and purposeful. There was no hesitation, no tentative first brush. This was the kind of kiss that possessed her, and she surrendered to it completely, yielding to the unspoken desire she had long secretly harbored.

Their lips moved in perfect sync, each one pushing and pulling as though their bodies had been waiting for this moment. His strong hands slid down to her backside, pulling her closer, his grip firm and possessive. She gasped softly against his mouth as her body pressed into him, and her thigh brushed against his hardness. The realization hit her like a spark igniting a flame. Everything about McKintrick was hard, from his chiseled abs to the stubborn, unyielding force of his personality. She realized that his very essence was a vast reservoir of those masculine energies that she appreciated so well. He was the deep end of those energies. These were uncharted waters. Ones that she had always longed to dive into, and perhaps the only place where she could truly swim freely.

She felt herself beginning to give in, her body softening against him, and instead of resisting, she leaned into the power of that surrender. There was control in submission, a quiet mastery of her femininity. Slowly, she began to sway her hips against him, her movements deliberate, teasing, drawing him in further with every shift of her body. His breath caught, but it was when she kissed him again, deep and slow, that the tension truly bloomed.

Then, she slowed herself. Her hips stilled, and she pulled back just enough to meet his gaze. Their eyes locked in a long, tender stare. Connection, a shared moment of vulnerability between two strong, unyielding people. And, for once, neither one was fighting anything. He lifted a hand and gently pushed a stray lock of hair from her face, the warmth of the gesture melting the space between them.

Who am I kidding? she thought, her heart thudding. *I can't compete with this strength. I don't even want to.* The sun warmed her shoulders, a quiet apology from nature for having led her to compete. There was strength carved into this man's face, more than she could summon in her entire body. She both revered and feared it. Yet, a deeper craving stirred within her. The desire to unleash the one force that could summon such strength - her femininity.

His lips found hers again, soft but firm, gentle but commanding. She tasted the sweetness of their sweat, warm and intoxicating, like a reminder of the effort they had poured into freeing the trailer and the desire now simmering between them. His hand slid to her neck, his fingers wrapping around it, not to restrict her, but to cradle her, and with a power she both respected and craved. The gentle pressure was a message, *I've got you.* The strength of his grip instantly dissolved any struggle to surrender. He was taking her, and she offered no objection.

His fingertips felt like strong lips on her neck and with her trust given, he pressed her backward with quiet control, laying her across the warm hood of the tractor. The heat of the sun-soaked metal against her back only heightened her awareness of every place he touched her. His fingers, skilled and purposeful, trailed down her body. They unfastened the single clasp on her Daisy Dukes, which slid down her legs effortlessly, catching briefly on her boots before falling to the ground.

The second they were gone, McKintrick's excitement raced when seeing her full wetness. Instantly, he was pressed against her, and instinctively, she arched to meet him. There was no hesitation, he thrusted forward. She gasped, breathless with realization, he was larger than she had imagined. For a fleeting moment, he almost overwhelmed her, teetering on the edge of too much. But then, her body yielded, succumbing to her own rising need, craving him with reckless surrender as he moved with purpose. Every deliberate motion whispered of his certainty. He already knew exactly how to unravel her, piece by piece.

The heat of his hand lingered at her neck, steady, claiming - a possessive weight that sent heat coursing through her. The valley of her breasts cradled his forearm as he thrust deeply, powerfully. This was a hard man, one shaped by a rugged existence, driven by the primal need. A man who *needed* to release within her. She felt that need in every movement, and she wanted to be the center of that focus, where all his masculine energy converged, pouring into her.

The thought alone made her pussy tighten and swell around him. Her body grasped him, clinging to him, drawing him in deeper. He swelled even more in response, hardening further with every squeeze from her lips. A bead of sweat rolled from his handsome face and dripped onto her nipples, sending shivers through Kayla. Her neck remained pinned under the weight of his working hands, but she could easily breathe. This was a dance of dominance and submission, a role that Kayla slid into effortlessly, like water droplets from a flower's petals dripping into a mountain stream.

His pace quickened, hips driving into her with relentless urgency. He groaned. McKintrick began to grind his teeth. The weight of his hand around her neck increased, adding pressure but never fear. She loved dancing along that exhilarating edge. He pulled her down onto him, anchoring himself inside of her. Kayla wondered if her body had been made to take him as his intensity consumed her, a heat radiating from her core as her swollen lips pulsed under his relentless thrusts.

Until - everything shifted. A dazzling brightness, almost spiritual, flooded her senses as he released her neck. He had grabbed both of her hips and pulled her onto him, remaining inside of her. Warmth spread through her body like a wave, as his release surged into her - full, pulsating, and undeniable. The dual sensation shattered her composure. He grabbed her rear, strong fingers sinking into her flesh as he pulled her tightly against him, anchoring her to his body. There was no escape, not that she wanted one. She surrendered fully, her legs wrapping around him, locking him inside her as he gritted his teeth and unleashed a deep, primal roar.

Her body reacted in kind. Her pussy twitched, shuddering with anticipation. Her breath twitched, and she began to unfurl like a slow, rolling storm. A moan escaped her lips, long and drawn-out, a sound she barely recognized as her own. She could not let go of him, would not let go. Her arms wrapped around his muscular frame, pulling herself onto him, riding him with a desperate hunger. His warmth filled her from the inside, while the sun's heat kissed her bare skin, her breasts rising and falling against him.

Her body gripped him with a rhythm all its own - tight, pulsing contractions like a rubber band snapping back to claim him, again and again. Her legs trembled, toes curling skyward as her pussy took over with waves of pleasure crashing through her. She cried out a long final screech, a sound that echoed off the barn walls and drifted across the rolling hills, heard only by the wind.

Exhausted yet again, she lay back on the tractor hood. The metal's warmth seeped into her skin as the sun had heated it long before their bodies claimed the area. Completely exposed, wearing nothing but boots, she felt him still inside her, his hardness lingering as if unwilling to part. With one final, deliberate thrust and a long grunt, he buried himself deeper, ensuring that every part of him stayed within her, a primitive and possessive act - a claim she silently welcomed.

Kayla let out a soft moan of appreciation, her eyes fluttering open to find him watching her. She smiled, her expression teasing and warm, as if to say, "Smartass". His lips curled into a grin, reflecting her satisfaction back to her.

~ ~

Within seconds, McKintrick was off the tractor, moving with the same ease and purpose he had during their struggle with the trailer. His soaked member jiggled in the breeze as mud sloshed beneath his boots. He pulled his overalls back up over his broad shoulders, the moment slipping seamlessly into the rhythm of farm life once more. But for Kayla, the moment lingered.

She lay there, sprawled across the warm hood of the tractor, her skin still buzzing from the heat of the sun and everything that had just happened. A dull ache of desire began to develop in his absence. The metal beneath her was comforting, grounding her in the present moment as she soaked in the afterglow of surrender and satisfaction. With a playful grin, she tilted her head toward the sky, then called out loudly enough for him to hear, "You gonna show me that house?"

For a moment, only the breeze answered her. Then, from the distance, she heard his voice - strong, deliberate. "No."

The rejection hung in the air, but only for a moment. His follow up words were more smooth than the pause that preceded them: "Gotta give you a reason to come back tomorrow."

She laughed, the sound bubbling up naturally as she pressed her hands to her lips. Of course, that was his answer. *McKintrick,* she thought with a mix of amusement and admiration. *You never know what you're gonna get.*

Dare to read what he's never shared aloud? Morgan's private stories await - subscribe to hear updates about them at www.*TheKnightOfRomance*.com

Beneath The Surface

Fresh, nostalgic, and laced with quiet temptation. The crisp, first taste sings in a setting where memory and reality blur. As the flavors deepen, a sweetness emerges, mirroring the tension between past innocence and newfound desire. And the finish? A whisper of truth and a teasing hint of mystery, leaving behind the lingering ache of what was - and what could be.

Suggested Pairings

Wine: Sauvignon Blanc (Loire Valley, France)

Cocktail: The Midnight Swim

Coffee: Dark Moon Espresso Tonic

Zero Proof: Moonlit Chai Cooler

Indulge Freely!
Morgan Knight

I've tucked the recipes for each intoxicating beverage safely at
www.*TheKnightOfRomance*.com

"Nooooo, it's too late," Noelle laughed, her voice bubbling with amusement. "You. Are. Ridiculous." She could not help but tease, though her tone carried a hint of admiration for his daring nature.

"Yep," Dustin shot back with a grin. "I am ridiculous. But tonight is too damn hot. And 'late' is relative." In an instant, he was off, disappearing into the fading light. Noelle could hear the rhythmic slap of his flip-flops against his heels, blending with the soft crunch of gravel beneath his feet. Their duet drifted away as he trotted down the trail toward the lake's edge.

Left in the quiet, Noelle remained, perched in the shotgun seat of Dustin's '87 open-top Jeep. She breathed in the warm evening air, savoring the peace. She'd been away far too long. Home. She'd forgotten the enchanting charm this place held. The hills surrounding the canyon wrapped the valley in a protective embrace, their peaks standing tall like ancient sentinels. Seems like fate always smiled on those who lived here.

And surely, fate had something to do with today, right? Both cell phones - dead. Charge cords? In another car. No CDs. No MP3. Not even an 80s cassette. Just an old, battered ghetto blaster strapped in the backseat like a rebellious child. Its FM tuner long lost, leaving it to stubbornly squawk out static-filled AM channels. A crackling "Summer Lovin'" had been drifting through the airwaves when they pulled up, and now the tune from Grease was set in Noelle's head. With all this familiar emotional energy floating around her, how could fate not be near?

The perfect end to the perfect day. Noelle's bikini, now dry but still clinging to her hips beneath her frayed denim cutoffs, felt like a second skin. She could not remember the last time that she had experienced a day like this. Perhaps when she was 16, maybe 17, she mused. There had been occasional moments spent on the lake since then, but nothing like today. This felt different. Restorative. Noelle inhaled deeply, letting the sweet nostalgia of the day wash over her, each breath pulling her back to a simpler time, to easier days.

In the distance, she heard it - *SPLASH!*. Dustin was in. His voice carried across the water, echoing back to her. "C'mon!" Noelle rolled her eyes and couldn't help but mock him silently, *"Now THAT'S a convincing argument."* But the truth was, did she really need persuading? Dustin, it turns out, was not the same Dustin of yesteryear.

Noelle's memories of him felt almost like a familiar troupe. She had placed Dustin in the friend zone back in junior high, a role he continued to play throughout high school. He was her comrade, her musketeer. They shared each other's victories and offered comfort during defeats. Of course, there were always those occasional "attempts" on Dustin's part, but they were innocent in nature, never anything worthy of prosecution.

The truth was that her physical attraction for Dustin had never seeded back then, and because of that, Noelle never had a row of lust to sow for him. But fate had, in its own way, granted them a series of emotional exchanges over the years, nurturing a connection deeper than most could ever dream. They had cultivated a bond, tending to that bond like a garden of understanding. She admired his courage, his audacity, his playful goofiness. But, the physical connection was always absent, and that fact, despite everything, had always saddened her. He had the heart of a lion in those days, but his wiry frame could not quite match the strength of his spirit.

Like fireflies, these memories flitted around Noelle as she unbuckled her seatbelt. Their glowing dance illuminated the moments of her past. She pulled the door handle, the Jeep's rusted hatch creaking in protest. She swung her leg out, stepped onto the earth, then looked up into the sky behind her shoulder. The moon had made his entrance. Enormous, dominating the sky and taking center stage. "Whoa," she muttered. "That's new."

Atop the embankment, Noelle felt as though Mr. Moon was so close she could almost reach out and touch him, perhaps just a simple tap on his cool, silvery shoulder. His charm lay in the way he reflected his own brilliance off the beautiful lake below, who seemed like a composed lady in her serene stillness. Without explanation, Noelle found herself caught in a celestial cocktail party, with Mr. Moon himself subtly petitioning for an introduction to Miss Lake. He indicated a palpable infatuation with her ripples, created by Dustin's splash. As the illusion began to fade, Noelle raised an eyebrow and muttered, "What the hell are you up to, Fate?"

Leaving the moon to play his part, Noelle began her trek down the embankment trail toward the lake. "Healing" was the only word that came to mind when she thought of the adventures that had led her here. These were the energies of her youth. They were now stirring within her once again, reminding her of who she was, what she had overcome, and where she was heading.

Water, boats, jet skis, fishing, tubing - these were the recreations of her developing years. But the town's connection to the lakes went much deeper than that. Much deeper. Their history included the worshiping practices of the Potowatomi along the shorelines, pioneers who fed and nourished themselves from the lakes, on up through thousands of marital ceremonies "in", "on", or "around" the lakes. This was a community that hosted generation after generation of people who held a nearly spiritual connection with those waters. How lucky could a girl get?

As Noelle continued her traipse, sights along the trail began to piece themselves into recognition, the curve in the path, the distinct row of trees, and the faint recollection of a rusted-out rowboat. Had she? Yes. She'd been here before. The realization rushed through her like a cascading waterfall. This was the spot where she and Dustin swam as budding teenagers. A hidden gem they'd stumbled upon while out riding bikes one day. She chuckled to herself, remembering how Dustin had tried to convince her to go skinny dipping. "Oh, the audacity," she murmured. *Still, not the worst idea,* she mused with a sly grin.

Before yesterday, there had been years, too many, really, since they had heard a word of the other. There was no grand explanation for why. People drift apart. No one person could be blamed for the distance. Just life. They hadn't even connected via social media. And then, two days ago, Fate intervened when Noelle recognized him.

Both she and Dustin had been swept into a fundraising event while visiting their individual parents on the same weekend. "The Black-Tie Paddle Wheel Cruise" was how the lake folks marketed the event, supposedly a fundraiser for the historic lighthouse, but everyone knew it was just an excuse to drink on a boat and flirt with neighbors. There were items auctioned off for the cause, but most attendees were well into their cups before the bidding even began.

On the auction block, one accolade towered above all others: a Men's NCAA Championship swimming trophy. The owner had signed it along with the rest of his swim team including Olympic gold medalist, Michael Phelps. For a community built around water recreation, this gem held bragging rights. Noelle's eyes drifted to the inscription card at the base: *"Graciously donated by Dustin Robertson."* She froze. Dustin? *Was this...THE Dustin?* A whirlwind of thoughts swirled within her. She was torn, caught in a tug-of-war of disbelief. *It can't be.* Then, *Can it?* Followed by, *No.* And finally, a questioning, *Really? Is it?*

Beside the trophy, Dustin's aunt had assembled a poster, a collage of amateur photos showcasing his achievements, each one more impressive than the last. For most of us, such a display would be embarrassing, but Dustin's laid-back demeanor prevented any sense of shame from overtaking him. Noelle scanned the photos, her recognition of him dawning slowly. He looked like a celebrity.

Years of college swimming had carved him into something formidable. His boyhood frame was now a testament to strength and discipline. His arms, once unremarkable, had flourished into sculpted lines of power, his shoulders so striking they carried their own quiet authority. And that V-shaped torso? A masterpiece of motion and muscle.

Then Noelle's gaze caught on something else - abs. Defined, undeniable. "Oh, holy hell. Actual abs," she nearly whispered, with her breath catching as she gawked at the photograph.

And then, across the room, she saw him.

Noelle understood at once why two elegantly dressed women clung to his presence, their laughter laced with the desire to be seen, to be chosen. But then, Dustin's eyes found hers. Instinctual. Inevitable.

The heat of his gaze touched her first, a slow warmth spreading over her skin before melting into that signature grin. With effortless charm, he excused himself, slipping from conversation like a magician shedding his chains. And as he freed himself from their laughter, their perfume, their elegant allure, a quiet thrill unfurled in Noelle's chest. In that moment, she acknowledged the undeniable power of a familiar connection. In that moment, he had chosen *her*.

With a playful, exaggerated sashay, Dustin crossed the space between them. Like a silent encore from their past, he took her hand and brushed a slow, deliberate kiss against the back of it.

"Good evening, my Queen," he murmured, mischief curling at the edges of his smile.

The words were an echo of junior high, an icebreaker wrapped in nostalgia. Noelle pressed her lips together, fighting the pull of a smile, just as she had all those years ago.

But who could resist? Laughter spilled forth, light and unguarded, as that old, familiar spark suddenly rekindled, like a match catching flame. The years, the distance, the unspoken word between them all dissolved into the warmth of a single, stolen moment.

The memory of those laughs faded into echoes as Noelle reached the trail's end, her steps carrying her toward the dock. The debate over skinny dipping lingered in the air. *Was that what he had in mind?*

He was *too* charming to swim with now - too distracting.

What were his intentions? Did he still carry a torch for her? And, more unsettling, was she now carrying one for him? The answer came swiftly, a quiet yet resolute *yes*. The thought sent a rush through her, wild and unbridled, kicking up dust in her mind like a herd of broncos charging across the plains.

As Noelle strolled toward the dock's edge, she took silent inventory of his abandoned clothing, each discarded piece a breadcrumb on the path to the water. T-shirt. Flip-flop #1. Baseball cap. She smirked, recalling their earlier banter. "That's not even a real team," she teased, despite knowing full well she had no idea, nor wouldn't even have been able to name the sport.

Her thoughts scattered as she spotted flip-flop #2. Another deduction from his clothing balance sheet. Then she stopped at the water's edge. *Hmm... no swim trunks on the ground.* Every item accounted for. Every piece a legitimate expense. Dustin was *not* skinny-dipping.

Such a good guy. And yet, for the briefest second, a pinprick of disappointment pressed against her, quick and fleeting. There, then gone.

She waded in, the warm water creeping higher, lapping at the hem of her knotted T-shirt. And then - nothing.

A sudden drop.

The lake swallowed her nearly whole, stealing her breath as she flailed, grasping for stability. Heart pounding, she scrambled back onto the ledge, sputtering. When she'd regained control of herself, she scanned across the moonlit waves and found his stupid, grinning head bobbing in her waves.

"What the *fuck?*" she yelled, her voice echoing off the canyon walls.

Laughter drifted back to her, carefree, boyish, and utterly unrepentant. He swam closer, his broad shoulders cutting through the water like the steady rudder of a ship. A part of her wanted to watch him move, to witness the raw power beneath the surface. *Unleash him,* she thought.

"Keep it down a little, huh? You want everyone waking up?" Dustin called out, his voice laced with quiet amusement.

"There's a drop-off," Noelle chirped back.

"Yeah, about six feet out," he replied, keeping himself afloat. Noelle glanced down at him, mesmerized by the fluid grace of his movements. *Daaaammmnn,* she thought. His ease in the water was hypnotic, almost elegant.

"It's dive-able," Dustin suggested, his tone playful.

"Dive-able?" Noelle raised an eyebrow.

"Yeah," he affirmed with a grin.

"That's not even a word," she shot back, shaking her head.

"It is now. I just made it up," he said with a confident shrug.

Noelle hesitated for a moment, unsure.

Dustin noticed and, with a teasing grin, added, "C'mon, this was your idea."

"SUGGESTION!" she snapped, her voice slicing through the air, sharpened with mock indignation.

"Shhh," he whispered, pressing a finger to his lips.

A pause. Then, in a voice laced with quiet intensity and wily undertones, he murmured, "Maybe don't *suggest* things to men of action."

The commanding tone in his voice sent a spark of interest through Noelle. *The New Justin?* She turned back toward the dock, pulling herself from the water in one smooth motion. As she peeled off her soaked shorts, a quiet thrill flickered beneath her skin, knowing Justin's eyes were on her. Let him look.

The moonlight traced the length of her legs, gilding them in silver. Smooth. Her T-shirt had come undone in the plunge; the knot lost to the water. She slipped it off, the damp fabric whispering against her skin as the night air kissed her bare shoulders. Droplets shimmered over her tan, catching the moon's reflection. Her breasts, slick and radiant beneath the lunar glow, rose and fell with her breath. A slow, knowing smile curved her lips.

"Thanks, Mr. Moon," she murmured, a private gratitude for nature's perfect lighting.

"It feels like a big leap, but it's really nothing," Dustin said with a grin.

Noelle stepped closer to the water's edge, her toes just grazing the dock. She could feel his eyes on her, probably judging her every move. That thought only added to the thrill, making the idea of pulling off an elegant dive all the more exhilarating. She took a breath and leaped.

When she resurfaced, her heart racing, Dustin's judgement was in. "Graceful," he said, his voice filled with genuine admiration.

Noelle shook her head, pushing the water from her ears, but she was satisfied with her dive. *Like riding a skateboard or bicycle*, she thought. Childhood skills always remained locked inside us.

"Did you hear me?" Dustin asked, his voice was steady.

"I heard you," she whispered.

Noelle's breath deepened. She could not help but wonder if Dustin could hear the rapid beat of her heart, pounding outside her chest. Her legs churned in the water. Their eyes met again, and they both shivered - nerves. The warmth of the water soothed those nerves, just slightly, as Dustin's arm moved around her waist. *Damn... those forearms*, Noelle thought. Dustin pulled her closer, and their thighs brushed against each other. Their legs churned together in fluid synchrony.

Water heightens the skin's alertness, intensifying the electric charge between them with even a simple touch. When Dustin brought his lips to hers, the rush surged through her. Noelle felt her lips swell under his kiss. Gently, his tongue sought hers, and she wrapped her arms around his broad shoulders. Waves kissed their cheeks, occasionally interrupting the rhythm of their lips and tongues. As her legs continued to churn, Noelle's thigh grazed him once more. *Whoa*, she thought, but before that single syllable could finish echoing within her, Dustin dipped beneath her arms.

"What the...?" she murmured in surprise. He swam underneath her. Noelle slowly came to wonder, *Is he embarrassed?*

Dustin surfaced several yards away, flipping onto his side to face her, flashing a grin. He called out, "C'mon," his voice playful yet persistent.

With a mischievous glint in his eyes, he swam backward toward a diving pontoon, keeping his gaze fixed on Noelle, but his pelvis below the waterline. *Yeah, maybe embarrassment,* Noelle thought with a faint smile. She couldn't help but feel a bit sorry for him. Embarrassed? She knew this was completely natural.

She, however, was not embarrassed. In fact, Noelle felt a quiet satisfaction at having that effect on him. She allowed herself a playful giggle, thinking, *My boobs do look good in this light,* before she began to swim after him. She knew he could easily outswim her. He could show off his mad skills, trying to impress her. But such insecurities never surfaced for him.

After climbing aboard the pontoon, the water rushed off her skin. The surface beneath her feet had changed since the diving pontoons of her youth. Gone were the garish green faux grass coverings. Now, the surface was smooth, rubbery, gentle on the feet, like a warm leather car-seat still holding the day's warmth. *These people must have money,* Noelle thought, noticing the pontoon's impressive amenities including a slide and diving board.

Fully aboard, she spotted Dustin standing behind the slide, poised at the diving board. She froze. *"Holy crap."* She had seen athletic bodies online and in photos, but never one in person - never in their full, prime condition. The sight of him took her breath away. Inspiring. Nearly divine. "Awe" was too short of a word to justify the impression. The swim had pumped his arm and shoulder muscles into their natural fullness, and his broad back seemed to stretch like wings, tapering down to a narrow, powerful waist. Noelle smiled; a warm feeling of pride washed over her. She was proud of the man he had become, almost as if she had helped raise him. In truth, she had. They both had a hand in raising each other, as all children do.

She sauntered toward him, intent on interrupting the playful dive he was preparing. Her hand reached up to touch his sculpted cheekbones, and she brought her lips to his, soft and tender. The kisses she planted were laced with a quiet seduction, meant to draw more from him.

But once again, and just as unexpectedly, Dustin leaped into the air. Another escape. The diving board's vibrations echoed through the canyon, a sign of the power behind his jump. His form - perfect, and his entrance into the water yielded a simple ripple.

Noelle was puzzled. *That's not embarrassment,* she thought. *That's something else.* Was this payback? Was he subconsciously nervous? Though the words eluded her, Noelle sensed on a deeper level that something was holding Dustin back. But she also knew they were both adults now. *What would it take to unleash the tiger she knew was inside him, but he continued resisting?*

Dustin swam beneath the diving platform, where the pontoons created a bubble of air below the platform. This was the perfect place for him to surface, take a breath, and chat with Noelle, to coax her back into the water. "C'mon," he whispered, his voice echoing against the steel floats above.

Noelle understood that this was a man who had thrived on competition since boyhood. Might she use that to her advantage? Years of unspoken desire would be her bait, and herself, now a fully formed woman, standing before him, would be the hook. With that, Noelle was going fishing.

"Not exactly the splash size I was expecting," she challenged.

Dustin laughed. "You think you can do better?"

Noelle smirked, her tone teasing yet suggestive. "Oh, yeah. I can make a HUGE...splash."

"Do it," he urged. "Maybe I'll stay under here to avoid getting hit by the force," he teased.

A mystical silence draped over the lake, thick and absolute, as if woven by Mr. Moon himself. Perhaps, at Fate's command.

But no jump came. No splash.

Only silence.

Dustin slipped from beneath the pontoon platform, water streaming from his skin as he surfaced. His voice, low and searching, cut through the stillness.

"Noelle?"

No reply.

A flicker of unease stirred in his chest. He climbed aboard, scanning the dim-lit expanse of the dock, the water, the shadows beyond.

"You okay?"

The night held its breath. Noelle was nowhere on board.

Dustin checked beneath the diving board. Nothing. Around the back of the slide. Nothing. His gaze swept over the pontoon, searching, until - there.

A clue.

In the far corner, Noelle's bikini lay in a careless heap, every last piece abandoned. The realization struck just as a sound reached him, a soft, teasing giggle. Above. His head snapped up, catching the faintest flicker of movement. Then, the telltale squeak of the slide's surface, a rush of motion, the blur of her bare skin twisting through the air. For a single heartbeat, he glimpsed her completely and breathtakingly free. Before - SPLASH! A tidal wave of water erupted, drenching everything in its wake.

When Noelle resurfaced, she reached for the pontoon platform, her doe eyes locking with Dustin's. She maintained her steady gaze on him as she dipped her face into the water, then resurfaced beneath the pontoon. Dustin scrambled above her; his movements frantic. A moment later, Noelle heard her reward: the sound of a zipper, an awkward step, and then...SPLASH!

She felt him before she saw him, approaching through the silent currents beneath her. Dustin surfaced under the pontoon with her, but no longer showing any signs of embarrassment, rejection, or exposure. Noelle had figured out the root of the tension between them, that invisible thread pulling tight and fraying at the edges. The issue was the past, lingering like a constant echo laced with fear. Fear of rejection. Residue from their younger years had been hovering in the space between them, Noelle understood now that this had been her fault.

Childhood is a landscape of oversights and regrets, shaped by the simple truth that we lacked the wisdom and means to set things right back then. Dustin needed certainty now. Not hints, not lingering glances, but undeniable confirmation that Noelle wanted him as fiercely as he had always wanted her. He was no longer a boy who could afford to go *halfway*. He was a man, accomplished and decisive. The hesitations of youth no longer ran in his blood. His duck and cover moves in the water were simply a strategy to maintain that edge, and Noelle appreciated that he could never abandon that competitive fire within himself. Not even for her.

Noelle's boldness had swept away the last of his lingering doubts. She saw it now. Dustin was a man who knew himself completely, the way elite athletes do. Physically. Emotionally. Mentally. There was no hesitation in him, no room for the shadows of childhood rejection to linger. That chapter had closed. And in freeing him, she had rewritten their story. The past dissolved, washed away like marks in the sand, leaving only the warmth of the present and the unwritten pages of their story yet to be told.

Their trembling returned, not from the cold, but from courage. That boldness crackled like a fire beneath their skin. Noelle's fingers curled around the pontoon's supports as she reached for him, her legs wrapping around his waist, drawing him near. Their lips met again; the kiss no longer playful but deep, urgent, consuming.

Her bare skin pressed against his. The warmth of his skin pressed into her, every inch of contact igniting something raw and electric. She felt the full strength of his body, undeniable and elemental, which should have overwhelmed her, but instead, she met it head-on. Her hand reached downward, finding him. Her touch, slow and deliberate. Gently, she held him in her hand, his size flirting with the edge of both stimulating and frightening. And in that moment, she realized - this was no mere man.

Dustin's powerful arms wrapped around Noelle. The look in his eyes told her to hold her breath. He pushed off, and they sank together, Noelle still wrapped around him. The sensation of his nakedness against hers, guiding through the water, felt almost supernatural. A wave of exhilaration and protectiveness surged through her, as Dustin guided them from beneath the pontoon, the water parting around them like a private world.

They rose from the water, droplets tumbling from their skin, catching the moonlight like falling stars. Dustin climbed the pontoon's ladder, his movements effortless, powerful. Noelle clung to him, her lips tracing the curve of his neck, tasting the warmth of him, the salt of the lake. Her gaze drifted downward, and in the silver glow, every ridge of his torso was carved into something almost unreal.

Damn, he looks like a myth in this light.

Before she could fully catch her breath, he began to lower her - slowly, deliberately. A silent promise woven into the motion. Even as they descended, she never questioned his strength. It surrounded her, unshakable, effortless, as though she weighed nothing at all, as though she belonged nowhere else but here.

In that breathless moment, the last remnants of childhood dissolved into the night. They were no longer just two souls playing in the water but something more, two bodies drawn together in a timeless, unspoken ritual beneath the moon's watchful eye.

She felt him - solid, undeniable - pressing against her, knocking softly at the edge of her desire. A silent invitation, potent enough to send a shiver cascading through her. Then, as her back met the cushioned floor of the pontoon, the gentle impact sent her forward, pressing her against him. And just like that, the space between them ceased to exist.

Noelle's eyes lifted to his, wide with longing, a silent plea woven with vulnerability. She was Jane to his Tarzan, drawn to the raw, untamed strength that radiated from him.

Their gazes tangled, the space between them humming with unspoken understanding. He lingered at her threshold, teasing, testing, his presence a slow-burning promise. Then, at last, his lips claimed hers - hungry, deliberate - before trailing downward, seeking the tender curve of her neck. She surrendered to the moment, lost in the exquisite tension and anticipation of what was to come.

With commanding certainty, Dustin's hips pressed forward, a shiver rippling through her as her body opened to him, welcoming, yielding. Her lower lips parted - a silent, instinctive invitation, a curtsy of surrender. Noelle's back arched, a sharp gasp spilling from her lips as he exhaled a low, primal sigh.

Relief hovered between them, tantalizingly close, but just out of reach. And in that unspoken moment, they understood, this was not just desire but a pursuit, a journey. Their eyes met - an agreement to chase that relief together, breath for breath, heartbeat for heartbeat, until they found it.

Dustin remained within her as he rolled them effortlessly, settling Noelle atop him. She had already measured his size and understood that this was only the beginning, a first step into something deeper, something more. There was more of him to take in, more of him to surrender to. His sculpted arms lifted her with ease, a seamless display of strength and control. He gave her body time - time to adjust, to mold around him, to learn him. Then, with a slow, deliberate descent, he guided her back down, a teasing rhythm, a deeper joining. A promise of more.

The rhythm unfolded, unhurried yet deliberate - a slow, intoxicating tease that stirred something primal within her. With each descent, she took more of him, her breath catching as pleasure coiled tighter, winding like a silk ribbon around her spine.

Every movement, every measured thrust, sent a wave of something deeper than desire - *gratitude*. Gratitude that he was claiming her. Filling her. Making her his.

Their pace quickened, a relentless force she both craved and barely endured. She teetered on the edge, caught between the staggering power of his upward thrusts and the intoxicating surrender to them. She ached for more, yet he pushed the limits of what she could take. Her lips clung to him, tightening, choking him in greedy defiance.

Dustin rolled them back over, again, and now met her with raw intensity. His rhythm escalated into deep, unrelenting slams. She was trapped - caged by pleasure, bound by the sheer force of him. His animalistic hunger had taken over, and she welcomed the beast that she had unchained, letting him consume her - mind, body, and soul.

Never had Noelle *needed* someone more. The promise of his afterglow fueled her own urgency, sending a wildfire through her veins, driving her body to rise, to meet him, to take him deeper still. Her back arched, her hips lifted - a silent offering, a desperate plea. Her fingers raked across his back, clawing at his shoulders, seeking an anchor as waves of sensation surged through her. She gasped, her body molding to his at last, surrendering. Her legs locked around him, a vice-like grip that left no escape. Not now. Not when she needed every inch of him. The movement tightened their connection, fusing their bodies, sending a slow, searing heat through her core.

And in that moment, she was his. Completely.

Noelle was close - *too* close. She knew he was too. Their voices tangled in the thick air, her moans weaving into his deep, guttural grunts. The rhythm between them surged, primal and unrelenting, each thrust a pounding drumbeat in a symphony of flesh and need. Deeper. Slam.

Harder. The bass of their bodies reverberated through her, shaking her to the core, sending her spiraling beyond control.

She whimpered, breathless, desperate, her fingernails biting into his skin as she pleaded,

"Please, Dustin... cum inside me."

Her words set something off inside him. A raw groan rumbled from his chest, vibrating through her, seeping into her skin. Then, his body tensed, muscles coiling like a drawn bow. His back arched, and in a rush of heat, he poured into her.

Noelle howled, her release colliding with his like a violent storm breaking over the sea.

CRAAAAAAAAAASH!

Her body clenched, convulsed, trapping him in a vice of unbearable pleasure.

Another wave - *CRAAASH!*

Her inner muscles spasmed, tightening, pulling, milking him, as the last remnants of control shattered around her.

CRASH!

Her legs locked around him, holding him deep, refusing to let go. Not yet. Not now. Not until every last tremor had passed.

The after tremors began. Like dominoes falling, each aftershock toppled into the next.

CRASH.

A quake of pleasure, raw and uncontrollable.

CRASH... Crash... crash...

The final tremors melted into stillness, their tangled moans dissolving into breathless silence. Her walls fluttered around him, reluctant to let go, instinctively holding, drawing *in* every last drop of him. Savoring him. Keeping him.

Noelle trembled, her body still humming with aftershocks. Dustin mirrored her, his breath uneven, his muscles slack with exhaustion. Their eyes locked, lingering, then flickered across each other's faces - drenched in sweat, flushed with pleasure. Slowly, exhausted smiles formed between them, unspoken gratitude woven into their gazes.

He leaned in, his lips finding hers in a kiss that was softer now, laced with tenderness. Noelle brushed a damp lock from his forehead, her fingertips trailing along his skin as if committing the moment to memory. He remained inside her, his weight settling atop her, warm and steady. There was no awkwardness, no rush to move, only the quiet satisfaction of bodies entwined, of years spent together leading to *this*.

Their smiles deepened, a shared understanding passing between them. And as Noelle gazed up at the night sky, she couldn't help but wonder, had their playful passion just conceived the next generation of lake lovers?

Morgan's pen has not stopped. His next letter waits - exclusive, personal, and only for those who dare subscribe at
www.*TheKnightOfRomance*.com

Memphis Momentum

This story pours like no other sultry Southern tale. An unexpected encounter on the Memphis trolley will find you in a dark, smoky, and irresistibly bold state. As the night unfolds, velvety layers highlight a Southern gentleman's steady charm which combines with the unique flavors of an Asian woman's unraveling resistance. The story feels well aged, comforting, yet dangerously tempting. The finish smolders with bittersweet longing, lingering like a touch too intoxicating to forget.

Suggested Pairings

Wine: Hermitage or Côte Rôtie, France

Cocktail: The Southern Seduction

Coffee: Vietnamese Egg Coffee

Zero Proof: Hibiscus Iced Tea with Honey & Lemon

Drift Away!
Morgan Knight

The taste of these stories does not have to end.
Find the beverage recipes at www.*TheKnightOfRomance*.com

"Hmmmm," Vanna giggled. She had only planned to maybe kiss him. But now? She wasn't so sure. She might already be too emotionally submerged. Too far in. And this is only the first date. Damn those inner resistance battles.

"Just a technicality," Shane said with a smirk, his tone effortlessly playful.

Matching his playful energy, she reached for the bedpost, gripping it with one hand. Using it as an anchor, she let her body sway, leaning into a slow, teasing swing. The movement only intensified the dull ache stirring inside her, but she couldn't resist the chance to mess with him.

"Screw you," she laughed. "Why'd you have to break my glasses?"

"Part of my *maaaadddddd* plan," Shane declared, exaggerating the words like a cartoon mad scientist as he settled into the fireside armchair.

~~~~~~~~~~~~~~~~~~~~~~~~~~

Vanna met Shane by accident, literally. Crowded trains tend to cause a whole host of inter-passenger mishaps, and the Memphis trolley was no exception. The incident unfolded quickly. She dropped her sunglasses. He stepped on them. Crushed 'em. Accidentally, of course. Later, she'd jokingly called their meeting one another, "introduction teamwork", but at the moment, all she could do was brush off his repeated apologies with a polite, "It's okay."

The exchange stirred quiet amusement among their fellow passengers. She knew Shane was walking the fine line between embarrassment and damage control, while she balanced somewhere between politeness and mild disappointment over her favorite shades.

The truth? Vanna was a mess.

Retail therapy had been the prescription for the day - necessary. Required, in fact. Maybe even doctor's orders. Her marriage was no longer just on the rocks, but that rock had shattered the hull and reduced the wood
~~~~~~~~~~~~~~~~~~~~~~~~~~

to wreckage. Years of watching something slam against the jagged cliffs of disrespect will do that.

Funny, she mused to herself. *"On the rocks" describes both a marriage and a glass of whiskey.* And damn, if whiskey didn't sound good right now.

She had signed the divorce papers earlier that week, keeping her composure despite her inner turmoil. Not because of *him,* but because of herself, because of her traditional Asian values. She felt they clashed against her true self. Those values dictated that a person remain in control of their faculties, regardless of inner challenges. No one ever just lashes out. But her heart begged her to be honest, to acknowledge the weight of what she had endured.

Still, a lighthearted conversation about broken sunglasses felt refreshing.

Shane, however, was insistent on replacing them.

"They're just cheap sunglasses," she assured him.

"Maybe so, but I broke them," he countered.

Is this guy hitting on me, she wondered. Not that she minded. In truth, she could use a little wooing.

As their playful debate continued, Vanna couldn't help but compare the man standing before her to the one she had recently escaped. The level of disrespect that she'd suffered at her ex's hands felt emotionally abusive. Years of it. The result had stripped her down to a fraction of her former self, leaving only a fragile shell. Years of emotional neglect and disrespect had chipped away at her until she barely recognized the woman staring back in the mirror. And with that, she felt justified in twisting whatever attention she received from men under the heading of "wooing". This was a need for Vanna. A need to feel wanted. Wanted in the manner that she'd felt prior to meeting the ex. Wanted in a way she hadn't felt in far too long.

But crossing that threshold to another man would not be easy. Nearly everything within her spoke ill of such a shift: her religion, her traditions, her family, her culture. But her sense of self spoke louder. That inner lioness roared, *FOUL.* She would no longer tolerate his indiscretions, his neglect, and as repeatedly stated, his disrespect. Vanna had made her decision. She would move forward, no matter the cost, wading through the uncertain waters of transition, no matter how cold or deep. She had no roadmap, no clear path back to her old self, nor any idea who the new Vanna might become.

But she knew this much. The memories of her ex, the good times, were just that. Memories. They were no longer foundational stones that she could stand on. The storms of change had torn through leaving nothing but emotional rubble. And staying there? Not an option. Yet, as she looked at the man before her, warmth flickered to life. Was it Shane's easy persistence? His sense of fun? His subtle, skillful persuasion? None of it mattered.

For the first time in a long time, she felt a little wooed. Whether she had projected the idea or not, she didn't know. She didn't care. Whether he meant to create the feeling or not, or whether she showed the feeling or not, was irrelevant. The feeling of being a little special was there for Vanna. And that feeling - that fleeting, an intoxicating reminder of what it was like to be desired, was what convinced her to disembark from the trolley with him at Beale Street.

~ ~

Stepping off the trolley with Shane didn't just feel right but also needed to happen. The lingering stares from the sunglasses dispute had grown mildly exhausting. Vanna knew that small emotional drains, if left unchecked, could add up quickly. And she wasn't about to let a silly accident and some judgmental glances from strangers chip away at the restorative peace she had built over a day of retail therapy.

She inhaled deeply, letting the warm, humid Memphis air settle over her like a weighted blanket. The air seemed laced with a calming agent.

Her tension continued to ease with every foot the trolly gained away from her. The sun's warmth contributed to the soothing effect, melting away the last traces of stress.

Finally, she looked up at Shane and for the first time was able to truly gather a decent gaze at him. Three words rushed into her mind: dashing, kind, and tall.

Dashing. Even in casual clothes, he was effortlessly put together, embodying the very essence of a Southern gentleman.

Kind. She winced at the simplicity of the word but relaxed when she realized how undeniably comfortable she felt around him.

Tall. Well, that was just plain obvious.

Vanna snickered. She had to tilt her head all the way back just to meet his gaze, the angle so extreme that the sunlight blinded her. She was unable to make out his full features as the sun glossed her eyes. She squinted, then chuckled. Vanna needed her sunglasses.

Shane held open the entrance door to a converted 1880s Victorian home, now an upscale eyewear boutique. Standing in the foyer, he motioned toward the displays with an easy confidence. "Please... choose."

Vanna hesitated, eyeing him with an amused grin. Small gestures of respect like this were already starting to pile up, drop by drop, into a cup of appreciation. Something about his presence, his energy, felt soothing.

Sensing her reluctance, Shane strolled deeper into the shop and announced casually, "Hell, maybe I'll find a pair for myself, too."

Vanna's grin twisted into a playful smirk. Without a word, she followed him inside, her gaze never leaving his.

Shane drifted off, giving Vanna her space. They each settled into their respective browsing areas, moving independently yet aware of the other's presence. Every so often, their gazes would meet in passing, quick glances, subtle observations.

The boutique had become a chessboard of sorts. When one moved, the other countered, their steps unfolded like a quiet, unspoken game. Shane slid his king's bishop toward the Ray-Ban case. Vanna nudged her queen's knight toward Oakley. *Was this flirting?* Vanna wasn't sure, but the thought made her stomach flutter.

Vanna then caught Shane's eye glancing at her left hand. His checking for an empty ring finger, sent a small thrill through her. And in return, she found herself unable to stop admiring the way his wavy hair fell effortlessly into place. There was a playful elegance to all of this, something straight out of a spy novel. *James Bond,* perhaps. And she, of course, *The Bond girl.*

Vanna leaned over a display case, eyeing a sleek pair of aviators. She squinted at the price tag.

A store associate approached. "May I help you?"

"Could I see those?" she asked, pointing.

He carefully flipped the sunglasses in his hand, revealing a bold engraving: CARTIER. Then, the price. $1,035.00. A sharp pang of embarrassment struck. Without missing a beat, she quickly waved it off.

"No, no - actually, the ones next to those."

The associate smoothly adjusted. "I apologize, ma'am."

From the corner of her eye, Vanna caught Shane watching. The corners of his mouth pulled into a teasing smirk before he turned away, feigning interest in another display case. Pawn to Polo.

Though neither player achieved a checkmate, Vanna ultimately settled on a modest pair, one that would not induce guilt when they inevitably met their demise. Shane chose a set as well, then quietly handled the payment.

She watched as he addressed the store associate by name, layering in polite "Sirs" and "Thank you's" with natural ease. All while thinking, *Politeness is sexy.*

But beneath his Southern gentleman charm, there was something else, something intangible. A quiet appealing strength. Ancient. Rooted. Her subconscious stirred. *I kinda wanna see that.*

Out on the sidewalk, Vanna's endless stream of "thank you's" were met with Shane's easy "you're welcome" and "no problem" In truth, she was stalling, throwing out desperate conversational lifelines to delay the inevitable moment of parting. She stood there, silently willing Shane to ask for her number. *Maybe an email. Anything. Please, God, anything.*

Hell, if he *really* went for it, she might even kiss him goodbye - *a light peck*, she noted to herself. *If he went for it.*

At her core, she was making a quiet, unspoken plea: *stay.* And she had a feeling he might be doing the same. Shane fumbled through a casual suggestion, "Lunch?".

Vanna accepted without hesitation. No objections. No deliberation. Motion granted.

~ ~

Lunch was fleeting, yet it fed her in ways far beyond the meal. Vanna caught herself staring at Shane, probably too often. She scolded herself internally, second-guessing every word. *Am I talking too much? Was that TMI?* Yet, she couldn't deny how much fun she was having. She felt light, almost girlish, swept up in something she hadn't let herself feel in years. The butterflies were a dead giveaway. *Yep, I like him.*

The way Shane affected her wasn't just about attraction but was more the way in which he carried himself. Calm, yet commanding. Effortless. She found herself wondering if he was the male equivalent of what so many men claimed they wanted in a woman: A lady in public, a whore in the bedroom. *Is that what I want from him?* The thought sent a quiet thrill through her. More surprising was the realization that she wanted to be that for him. She had simply never given herself permission before. But now?

The idea felt... right. Intimate, in a way she had never allowed herself to explore.

Somewhere between teasing glances and easy conversation, Vanna learned more about Shane's heritage. She had been correct, he was the rarely unearthed true Southern Gentlemen, one who authenticated words like *honor* and *truth*. The kind who didn't just say the words but lived them. The declaration of these ideals wooed her even further, leaving Vanna struggling to conceal the goosebumps rising along her arms.

She shared her story, too. Newly divorced. Grew up in Cambodia. Witnessed war tragedies she'd rather forget. Vanna had long suspected that this was why she gravitated toward men who made her feel protected. "Call 'em daddy issues if you want," she told Shane, then added, "probably what initially attracted me to my ex." But as she explained, he had been nothing more than an imposter of those ideals she held dear.

For the first time, she dared to say it out loud, she was struggling to move on. Not because of him. But, because of the promises she had made. She had built her life on the principles of honor, loyalty, and duty, and now she was forcing herself to accept that letting go of her marriage did not mean letting go of those values.

Shane listened patiently, offering quiet reassurances. "In your own time," he told her. "You'll make the moves you need to."

Almost as an afterthought, Vanna admitted, "This is actually my first date since the divorce."

Shane's eyebrows lifted. "This is a date?"

Vanna shot him a questioning stare, one brow arched. A slow, teasing smirk spread across his face. "This isn't a date." His voice dipped lower. "I'll show you a date." His grin. His gaze. The way he looked at her, like mischief, and adventure, and a whole lot of trouble were waiting just behind his next move.

Heat flared between her thighs. Without breaking eye contact, she grabbed the lunch receipt, scrawled her number across the back, and slid it toward him with quiet, unspoken intent. The confidence of an enchantress. The challenge of a woman who knew exactly what she wanted.

~ ~

Walking home was impossible. Vanna floated. Butterflies lifted her with every step, the weight of her shopping bags reduced to mere ounces. Passing a well-known BBQ joint, she laughed at the bold slogan plastered across its window: "Put some South in your mouth."

Her inner voice howled a comical, *HELL YEAH!* And just like that, a fantasy took hold, something that had not happened in years. She pictured herself in heels and a short skirt, straddling Shane's upper torso. His arms and legs pinned to the bed by her knees and legs, comfortably restrained. The sight of her glory so close yet just out of reach, taunting him, teasing him, until his need to taste her consumed him entirely.

She imagined looking down, locking eyes with him, those ocean-blue depths framed between her thighs. Watching his lips make out with hers until her body arched in surrender. The image sent a slow, curling heat through her. Then, just as suddenly, a wave of hesitation crashed over her.

Doubt was biologically ingrained in Vanna; a silent inheritance she had spent her life carrying. Frustration flared. She resented how her Asian heritage had always chained her to ideals that refused to account for the injustices she had endured. But then, a realization surfaced, kicking its way to the top of her consciousness. That realization surfaced, took a deep breath, and whispered her truth, *You are not just Cambodian. You are an American woman. Reinvent yourself.* The words felt like a key turning inside her. A weight lifted. For years, she had vowed to release the parts of her upbringing that held her back. And now? A major block had just cracked.

There would still be remnants, echoes of old fears, but she had made herself a promise, and she vowed to keep it. Vanna let out a breath, then smirked. "Yep. I'm American. Hell, I might even be a Southerner." The mix of raw desire and newfound freedom propelled her to pull out her phone. She typed a simple message: "Thank you for lunch...and the glasses."

Innocent enough. But the second she hit send, her pulse quickened. She found herself glancing at her phone again and again, waiting for the screen to light up. The moment she walked through her front door, a PING rang out. She snatched up the phone.

Shane: "Requiring dinner with you tomorrow night."

She smiled. Traditional Southern gentlemen walk that line between respect and a commanding presence better than most. A thrill ran through her, hot and electric, followed by twenty-four hours of anticipation. She surrendered to it, thinking, *Hell, I might even kiss him.*

Vanna sat up and tipped her shopping bags over, spilling the spoils of her retail therapy onto the ottoman. Amid the pile of fabric and receipts, one unmistakable jewel stood out, a finely clothed sunglasses case. The lettering gleamed back at her.

CARTIER

Her stomach flipped. She leaned back against the couch, a little dizzy from the realization. "Daaaaamn." She exhaled, shaking her head, "He's good. He's *REALLY* good."

~ ~

Shane had told Vanna he'd meet her outside Paulette's, a Southern-style restaurant nestled inside The River Inn of Harbor Town. The restaurant was on the first floor while gorgeous, antebellum-style hotel rooms with a twist of modern flair stacked themselves vertically above the dining room. The place mirrored Shane's own warmth and charm.

Arriving early, Vanna parked a few rows from the entrance and took a moment to observe. She watched as couples came and went. The men dressed sharply, their hands naturally finding the smalls of their dates' backs guiding them into the restaurant. She admired the quiet acts of chivalry, the effortless way they held doors open, the subtle gestures of care.

She liked that. She wanted that. Still, she waited. Her cautious nature demanded confirmation. She knew herself well, how easily she could get swept up in first impressions. *Was he as handsome as she remembered? As funny? As warm? As protective?* The foundation of attraction was there, solid as stone. But yesterday had been a whirlwind of shopping, sunglasses, and lunch. A sensory tornado. She needed a moment of stillness to know, just a fragment of certainty.

Still, she had dressed for the caper, just in case, with the little black dress as her accomplice along with the natural smoothness of her legs, another trusted partner in crime. Shoe store owners adored her for those legs. Their daring, hard-to-sell heels never looked better than they did on her. Most women relied on their legs to highlight the elegance of their shoes. But with Vanna? The rule was reversed. Just as the perfect frame enhances a masterpiece, her heels only served to intensify the allure of her legs. And they were, undeniably, a work of art.

Though she had dressed for success, Vanna still wanted one more sign, one last seed of evidence to confirm her attraction to him. Moving forward is hard, she reasoned. Was a final consideration of chemistry really too much to ask?

She replayed their moments from the sunglasses shop, the playful glances, the effortless humor, the way his boldness ran parallel with his charm. Even his ridiculous joke about DJ-ing, a not-so-subtle reference to how women pleasure themselves, had made her laugh in a way she hadn't in years. Everything was all so freeing. His effortless charm and quiet strength were a shelter she hadn't realized she craved, just the thought of it sent a slow, lingering heat through her. Would he still be what she remembered? Or had she been projecting the entire time? The doubt stirred, momentarily tugging at the ever-present struggle of moving on.

Finally, she saw him, and the question evaporated. Shane moved with effortless confidence, his stride both athletic and purposeful. Even beneath his sports coat, his broad shoulders hinted at strength, not just physical, but a quiet power that could command a room or a battlefield. *Well-rounded shoulders,* she mused, *and likely culturally well rounded, too. Probably well-traveled, as well.* Sharp cheekbones. Hunter eyes that held both intensity and kindness. Yes, this was walking, breathing handsomeness, and any lingering hesitation she had instantly dissolved.

Vanna stepped out of the car. The first click of her heels against the pavement sent a spark through her. She had chosen well. Her outfit was simple, elegant, and teasing. Just enough to reintroduce herself to the world. A quiet giggle escaped as she realized, those same heel clicks might as well have been a mating call.

Shane stood outside the entrance, waiting. He smiled, and with effortless grace, he held the door open for her, an invitation for her to consider the possibilities.

~ ~

Inside, the restaurant's elegance embraced her. The warm opulent décor felt like a quiet reassurance, an unspoken promise that, for tonight, troubles could wait at the door. The maître d' led them to a secluded corner booth, its plush red cushions more reminiscent of a Civil War-era chaise lounge than a customary booth. Vanna scooted in, expecting Shane to take the seat across from her. Instead, he slid in beside her.

"This is different," she remarked, gesturing toward the booth but meaning his choice of seating. Still, she didn't mind. She didn't mind at all.

Conversation flowed as effortlessly as the wine flights, with an impressive selection of vintners to choose from. She opted for sweet, while he chose dry. The charcuterie board arrived, and with it, a mischievous spark. Laughter spilled between them as they uncorked their juvenile sides, reshaping the board's offerings into cheeky little spectacles - two olives for breasts, a pickle placed with deliberate absurdity. Genuine pleasure flowed from the wine through their shared ridiculousness. This was easy.

Their shared humor felt like a playful rebellion against the restaurant's refined atmosphere, as if they had created their own private world with a fog of comfort and intimacy settling around their table. His periodic hunter stares flirted with her doe-like eyes, just as effortlessly as their conversation flowed. And, with every glance, every sip, every teasing remark, Vanna's longing grew.

She turned away to take a slow sip of wine. When she turned back, Shane's fingers were already there, brushing her chin, tilting her face toward his. Her breath caught. His gaze softened as she let her eyes flutter closed. Then, the warmth of his lips met hers, steady and unhurried. She tasted the richness of berries, and the weight of confidence. A quiet hunger stirred. She parted her lips, inviting him deeper, silently asking his tongue to sway with hers.

But he did not rush. He held back. Not from hesitation, but something else. She felt a quiet restraint, a respect for the emotions still settling inside her. And somehow, that restraint, his patience, made her want him even more.

The room softened into a welcoming haze. With Shane beside her, even the décor felt warmer, more inviting. Their kisses continued, interrupted only by fragments of conversation and slow sips of wine. The moment flowed through Vanna like a drug, warming her from the inside. She needed this. There was no danger here, only a deep, unmistakable sense of safety. This was intoxicating, this feeling of freedom, of permission, to unleash the audacity that had always simmered beneath her surface.

Their lips met again, and the kiss unraveled into slow, teasing hand play. Shane lifted her fingertips to his mouth, paying reverent attention to each one, his lips deliberate, sensual. Then, with devastating precision, he slid his tongue between her middle and index fingers. The suggestive sensation ignited something primal within her. The memory of the fantasy she had yesterday flared to life, playing in her mind like a forbidden film reel. She remembered straddling Shane, looking down into his deep blue eyes while he tasted her, repeatedly bringing her to her edge.

She exhaled slowly, steadying herself. Then, she reciprocated. Vanna took his hand, guiding his index finger along the inner rim of her wine glass. She tipped it forward just enough for him to feel the intoxicating wetness. His fingertip emerged slick with remnants of her Riesling. Holding his gaze, she slowly wrapped her lips around him.

Shane's head tilted back slightly, his eyes rolling shut, a quiet groan slipping from his throat. Vanna relished in the power. Emboldened, she let her manicured nails drift lower, delicately tracing the hard swell growing beneath his trousers. She felt him stiffen. He was ready. The seduction was seamless, instinctual, two bodies melting into their roles with effortless ease.

The heat between them thickened, the air turning electric. And just when she thought she might drown in such an atmosphere, a flicker of nervousness gripped her. Vanna inhaled sharply, then suddenly excused herself, slipping away to the ladies' room.

~ ~

Even here, in the privacy of the dimly lit restroom, the excitement clung to her like steam. She pressed her hands to the counter, steadying herself. "Okay... we kissed. We made out." The words, spoken aloud, sent another pulse of desire coursing through her. She wanted him. All of him. But then, the ghost from the past surfaced within her - the ex.

She met her own gaze in the mirror. *If you do this, there's no going back.* For a fraction of a second, she hesitated. And then, with a quiet exhale, she released the rope that had tethered her to the past. She watched as the ex's memory slipped below the surface, swallowed by the waves of time. He'd had his chances. Multiple chances. The guilt that once gripped her over betraying her commitment...betraying her own values...simply washed away with him.

And Vanna? She was riding a new wave now. A wave of freedom. A wave of an American woman who had chosen her own destiny. Standing before the mirror, she whispered her truth aloud, "I. Want. Shane." But she wanted something else, too. Control. Vanna realized that Shane was the only man who could give that back to her, by letting her take control when she wanted to. He wasn't a pushover. He was mannered, disciplined, and steady. She could push against him and feel her own power return to her, piece by piece, until the moment she decided to unleash him.

She would take him to the edge, reclaiming herself along the way, and then, she would step back and feel the explosion when things ultimately ignited between them. Her pulse quickened. She inhaled and let her energy release into the room. A slow turn in front of the mirror, and a final approving glance before she turned toward the door, ready to move on with her life.

As she crossed the lobby, her lips curled into a curious smile. Shane was not at the table but waiting for her in the lobby. Their bill? Paid. Before she questioned him, he closed the space between them, lifting her chin with those strong fingers once more, as his lips met hers. Warm and confident, still. Unhurried. Their tongues teased, a public slow dance of anticipation, until she heard a distinct sound, a soft *clank*. Metal against metal. Something cool and solid was in his hand. Vanna pulled back just enough to look at him. Shane met her gaze, his own stare laced with meaning. In her absence, Shand had gotten a room.

~ ~ ~ ~ ~ ~ ~ ~ ~ ~ ~ ~ ~ ~ ~ ~ ~ ~

The inn's arched stairway led them to the first door on the second floor, directly above the lobby and restaurant. The proximity to others only deepened Vanna's sense of safety. She was all in. Still, she could not resist teasing him, "Mighty presumptuous, sir."

Shane's response was quiet, raw, and honest, "I just need privacy, with you."

At the door, Vanna playfully plucked the key from his hand, pressing it firmly against his chest, "Allow me."

Shane's lips curled into a slow, approving smile, "You're in charge."

His words melted into her, pooling warmth in places she hadn't felt in years. She rewarded his patience by slipping her arms around his neck, pulling him down into a kiss. The key clanked against the old-fashioned chain, trying to find the entrance to the lock. *Foreshadowing?* Vanna mused.

Then, the handle turned. The door swung open, and they tumbled inside, a flurry of grasping hands, tangled limbs, and desperate lips. Shane's sport coat hit the floor within seconds. Vanna's hands moved with purpose, unbuttoning his shirt just enough to slip her manicured hands inside, *Oh my god, those shoulders are for real.* Her fingers skimmed lower, *Pectorals, too?* A rush of heat flooded through her.

"God, you feel good," she murmured, her hair falling in wild waves around her face. She wanted him more than she had imagined.

Their kisses turned reckless. A beautiful mess of lips, teeth, and hunger. Shane seized her wrists in one hand, gently locking them behind her back. Still, she reached upward for more of his lips. More of him.

With effortless strength, he spun her, guiding her toward the bed. Suddenly, she landed on her back. Her legs instinctively parted. A heartbeat later he was on top of her. She wrapped her beautiful legs around him. His weight. His strength. The sheer presence of him pressing against her. Security. Vanna exhaled a shaky breath, swallowed whole by the sensation. There was no defense against this level of security and wanting. And for the first time in a long time, she didn't want one.

Through his pants and her thong, she could feel his hardness against her. Vanna felt Shane instinctively and gently thrust against her. Their tongues and lips persisted in their joyful recreation. Vanna reached down to feel him. Her hand slid along his abdominals and weaved a way past his belt. She seized him. Vanna felt Shane's entire body melt against her, as he thrusted into her fist. Shane unbuckled himself. Vanna unbuttoned his pants and whisked his zipper down. He was out and lying against her. The only thing separating him from her was the thin, see-through fabric of Vanna's tiny thong.

Another thrust erupted from him as Shane moved his hand to her tiny hips. He pulled her upward against him. Vanna looked downward in adornment as she witnessed what she truly wanted resting against her lightly veiled jewel. He pulled her against him, again, only this time, his thumb had moved the safety net of her thong to one side. Vanna felt the length of his shaft slide against her, coating him in her excitement. Shane resisted piercing her but continued thrusting his length against her natural grooves. With each thrust, her clit was struck by his initial tip which was then smoothed over by the remaining length of his hardness, guiding along her.

Vanna rolled to the side, bringing Shane with her. She now rested on top of him. Her hair clouded her vision as much as passion clouded her mind. She seized him with her hand again and moved her mouth down to accept him. Vanna was hungry for him. She wanted him inside her in one way or another. Her restraint for not fucking him at this point was holding on by a thread. She was playing with her own control, and building him up, simultaneously.

Vanna jumped on top of him. Shane stood up, then picked her up. He stood there suspending Vanna above him as her arms and legs reached for him, wrapping around him in her descent. Vanna loved the difference in their sizes. She smothered him in lustful kisses and went so far as to lick his cheek. While carrying her, he meandered their way across the room with his drawn down trousers cuffing his ankles like linen leg shackles.

She felt his hardness alongside her again and pulled herself more tightly against him, savoring the grind. His backside landed them on the chaise davenport. Vanna took immediate control and seized him in her hand. She pulled her panties to the side with her free hand and teased herself with the tip of his throbbingness. Vanna could feel his pulse in her hand. She arched backwards, locking her legs around him. She knew Shane had a front row seat to her entire treasure which thrilled her even more. The fact that he could compose himself, restrain himself under such conditions, proved she'd chosen the right man. Vanna felt that somehow, he was allowing her to retrieve her lost sense of control, but she knew that he could not take much more, nor could she.

Vanna seized the base of his hardness and traced the outline of her lips, taking time to thoroughly color the northside of her clit with several passes. She felt transported. Vanna wanted to feel the weight, maybe the beginning stage of her lips being parted, but not actually pierced. She stood up and firmly planted her feet on the carpet. Her heels added the perfect amount of height to accomplish the maneuver. She lightly lowered herself onto him, just enough to feel pressure. Vanna reasoned that it was barely even the tip, if that.

She remained there, savoring the sensation of heat and his bulkiness. She watched as perspiration from holding back accumulated on his lower lip. *I can barely hold back myself*, Vanna acknowledged to herself. She sat atop him, watching his eyes roll around as if he were inebriated. She began to faintly bounce against him repeatedly, adoring the sweet flavor of the initial push and potential full parting of her lips. "God, I wanna go deeper", she whispered.

She looked down to gauge her depth. Their eyes met. He remained motionless, panting. She asked with wonder, "Are we...?", and looked for supportive confirmation.

With a sweet acknowledgement of letting her take the situation as far as she could, he gasped, "Look".

In her dance of delight, she had pulled a significant portion of Shane inside of her. His warm assertion confirmed for her that he would always tell her the truth, "I think it's safe to say that you're fucking me right now". The evidence was there for both to see. She re-examined the proof, the lovely sight of her lips and him inside of her. Vanna peered at Shane as she beamed a concoction of embarrassment and delight. She realized that she had gone as far as she could. Her control was back within her grasp, and a bridge had been crossed. She was free. Free to be whatever and whoever she wanted to be.

As a victory lap, Vanna smiled again at Shane. She replied, "Yeah...you're right." Then, maintained her locked gaze on him, and surrendered her previous position, by releasing herself, arching her back, and accepting all of Shane inside of her. His size overwhelmed her, and her moan overwhelmed him. His leash was off.

Shane stood up, carrying her while her lips and legs locked around him. He remained inside of Vanna as he carried her. He held her against him, as he lay her down on the carpet. The speed of the maneuver was breathtaking. She felt the plushness of the floor against her now nearly naked body. Shane drove the full weight of his mass inside of her. The force of his thrust pushed his pelvis against her clit. This duo combination overwhelmed Vanna as she arched her back again and again. She was being taken, and he was almost unbearable to take, but the thrill overrode any temporary discomfort. Shane was a master of straddling the line between pleasure and pain. Vanna began moaning, which accelerated his excitement. Their voices and breaths intertwined with one another.

Vanna gasped, "I'm building".

She could feel Shane building as well, as her tightness could accurately gauge his hardness. She threw her legs around him, feeling her heels dig into the power of his buttocks which continuously flexed against her. Each thrust resulted in another pelvic slam against her clit. Vanna was near. Shane followed right behind her. She pulled herself against him, as she felt herself begin to release, not allowing him to pull back. He escaped for a simple moment before his final push. The thrust remained with her, pushing her backwards. She could feel her lips sputtering against his mass as she held on. The room spun. She felt his warmth flooding into her. Her toes curled. Her back continued arching. Vanna could do nothing but hold on as their bodies released together. Sputtering. She was wrapped so tight around his cock and her legs so tight around his backside, that there would be no means of escaping. Shane growled. The animalistic nature of his release delighted her, a sound she'd never heard. His genuine tone reinforced simply how much Shane desired her.

Their mutual dance of tingles, throbs, and sputtering spasms continued as they descended together. Shane brought his tongue and lips to hers. Vanna's mouth accepted the invitation. Shane rolled the two of them over without escaping her. She rested on top of his chest in a delightful daze trying to recapture her breath, feeling the dull ache as he rested within her.

Shane began mumbling, but what he said, she could not decipher. Vanna hushed him by placing a light finger over his lips, then proclaimed through her exhaustion, "I have never...been so happy...", another gasp and a giggle, "to have my sunglasses broken".

Morgan's pen hasn't stopped. His next letter waits - exclusive, personal, and only for those who dare subscribe at www.*TheKnightOfRomance*.com

His Place, Her Rules

"It's open." His voice, rich and steady, rumbled through the solid door.

Brooke's fingers hovered over the antique knob, her pulse skimming just beneath her skin. But she didn't turn it. Not yet. An electrifying question flared in her mind, stopping her in place. *Would this be as good as she imagined?*

She'd already labeled this a "swipe right" relationship, an attraction that had deepened through a week of teasing texts and carefully curated photos. But she knew herself too well. Her mind was a stage where romance and fantasy performed on an endless loop, often outshining reality.

David's messages were compelling. Sweet, yet sharpened with an edge. Compliments delivered with precision, tempered by an unapologetic bluntness when necessary. *Boundaries are attractive.* Their exchanges crackled with something raw and unfiltered, like a late-night jazz riff. His words, steeped in confidence, poured into her like a strong, intoxicating brew. And now, standing on his doorstep, her cup of curiosity overflowed. But for some reason, hesitation loomed.

When they spoke and joked, David was never crude, never angling for nudes. Never returning them, either. He was, in a word, *forthright*, a quality that felt refreshing. Their playful banter had started with pure competition, each pushing the other, testing limits. But Brooke's attraction to him ran deeper. With David, there was no guessing, no reading between the lines. He possessed a rare kind of intellect, one that could track down her femininity with unnerving precision, leaving her nowhere to hide. Her competitive nature bristled at his skill, but something more honest within her thrived under his mastery. He kept her out of her head...in the moment, engaged. So far, she had not experienced a single drop of her toxic emotional fog that so often clouds the start of something new.

David had passed every test she'd unknowingly thrown at him. He succeeded by never taking Brooke's bait. And then, he received bonus points by never calling her out for such social violations. Somehow, David intuitively understood that women need to test men. They need verification that he is who he says he is. Each time Brooke found herself challenging David in such a way, he never faltered, raising her trust levels. And though Brook had never been one for games, experience had taught her that sometimes they were necessary. Too many times, she'd fallen for boys in men's clothing which was now shaping the way she navigated attraction.

A few years had passed since she felt nervous anticipation like this though - the giddy swell of something new. Years ago, she had buried similar feelings beneath a blaze of false hopes, betrayals, and outright lies. But, twice now, the delicate flutters she'd felt for David had thickened into something heavier, something hot and undeniable. What began as a playful joke had evolved - one teasing remark, a flirty retort, an escalation of intensity until their messages coiled into dangerous, thrilling territory, saying "If I were there, I'd..." Electric shivers ran through her spine, she knew how those sentences end.

One evening, Brooke scrolled through an old chat, retracing each playful jab and charged reply. The temperature of their exchange had climbed degree by degree until, at last, her fingertips had been persuaded to extinguish the flames herself. A confession she later boldly shared with David.

His response? Not shock. Not discomfort. Just acceptance. Appreciation. And with that, any lingering embarrassment dissolved, replaced by something far more dangerous. Their next conversation burned even hotter, pushing past teasing into the realm of raw, unfiltered fantasy.

She revealed her thirst for domination, how she never understood why a woman would resist being tamed. But, by the right guy.

"Who wouldn't want to be lusted after by someone that you lusted after?", she told David.

And with him, she felt those seeds of desire sinking deep, rooting themselves in the fertile soil of her imagination.

Now, here she stood. Outside his door. Perched on the fragile embankment where reality meets fantasy, where expectation tangles with possibility. If she stepped forward, if she jumped, would those worlds collide? Would they merge into something tangible, something real? The tension of that question had been gripping her for days. And now, hesitation pinned her in place.

But, if she lingered there too long, David would have to come to the door. He would have to see her falter, soothe her nerves. The moment he did, the fantasy would dissolve. She would not be the potent, untouchable femme she knew resided within her, but just another nervous girl, lost in the overwhelming weight of her own emotions.

A draft stirred through the hall corridor. A blend of soothing warmth swirled with elegant coolness, then rushed over her ankles, washed between her legs, and glided up her hips. The comforting air current dissipated once it reached her breasts. But a wake trailed behind the motion, creating small waves that crashed against her torso. With them, Brooke heard an echo. An awakening. A voice. The sound of her authentic self. The lusty, feminine expressionist, whispered,"*Ennnchaaaaannnntresss*". Nothing more was said. Just a word. Just an invitation. She remained motionless as the voice trailed into the echoes with the remnants of the draft.

A moment passed. Then, a rush of energy swelled within Brooke, vibrant and unshakable - cascading over her like waters from a warm bath, washing away any concepts of who she was not, and rinsing away years of self-doubt. Beneath everything, only *she* remained - potent and untamed, swaying with her native vibrance. She appreciated rediscovering the power of her femininity, and, like a kid with a new toy, she wanted to play. What emotions might be waiting on the other side of that door, she did not know. But she was excited to find out. And with that, she turned the knob.

~ ~

The door eased open, propelled by the faintest push. Chicago apartments are like that. Years of foundational settling and shifting throw the doors and windows out of alignment. A burst of warmth spilled from inside, rolling over her bare legs as the sharp tap of her heels punctuated the quiet foyer. *Heels?* she mused, smirking. *I must really like this guy if I changed into heels.*

She stepped into the dimly lit living room, slipping off her coat with a slow, deliberate movement before draping it neatly over her arms along with her purse. The steady rhythm of her heels on hardwood fueled her confidence, a sharp contrast to the hesitation she'd felt just a minute ago.

Then, she saw him. David. Seated in a sleek leather chair, his silhouette cut against the amber glow of an Edison bulb. Her stomach fluttered, that delicious mix of excitement and anticipation curling into a smirk on her lips.

He was dressed with intention. Slim-fit slacks, a crisp business shirt - French cuffs, even. Rolled just enough to hint at forearms that did more than type. His posture exuded quiet authority; one leg casually hiked over the other's knee in that effortlessly masculine way. The kind of stance that, if a woman tried to match in a short skirt, would leave her second-guessing every angle.

Brooke exhaled slowly. She was exactly where she wanted to be.

The ice *clinked* in David's glass as he took a slow sip of his añejo. The rich scent of aged tequila curled into the warm air, folding into the already simmering atmosphere. Even from across the room, Brooke could nearly taste the smoky sweetness lingering on his lips. A jolt flipped through her, a flash of memory, vivid and reckless. Spring break. Cancun. A crowded bar. She had licked the last drops of tequila from a stranger's lips, while gently grabbing him in public. Her teeth nibbled on his lower lip before she'd pulled away, leaving him stunned in the neon haze. No words. No second glance. Just the lingering heat of her audacity.

That same energy surged through her, now. A rediscovered piece of herself, stirred awake by the low-lit seduction of David's apartment. The seductive atmosphere hung around her like a fine mist, thick and intoxicating. She exhaled slowly, her pulse hammering in her throat. *How the fuck does he do this?* she wondered, *Nothing's even happened yet, and I'm already wet.*

She paused on seeing him, aligning her eyesight with his direction.

Then she spoke, soft and deliberate, "What do you want?" Her voice was smooth and teasing. Her natural competitiveness at play. But the authority in her own tone surprised even her. *Damn.* She almost laughed. *I sound like a high-class call girl.* The thought amused her as she joked with herself, *I would make a reaaaalllyyyy good high-class call girl.*

David paused. Then, his answer landed, matching Brooke's deliberateness, "Dance", he said. No explanation. No embellishment. Just a single, confident command.

Brooke hesitated, "...Without any music?" she challenged, arching a brow.

The pause stretched between them, electric. "Dance," he repeated. Unwavering. Something in his voice, calm, patient, and utterly sure made her fumble.

"I could, um... open my phone... or Spotify and ... "

He interrupted. Softly. "Dance." His voice had dropped to a whispering command, cloaked in velvet.

Hmm. Was this exchange a dance? Brooke wondered. She had stumbled on the first steps of whatever waltz they were playing, but the choreography of this game was second nature to her. She knew the steps. More importantly, she knew that she knew the steps.

Yes. Seduction was a dance - a ritualistic, untamed tribal tango where femininity lures virility into a mystical and hypnotic play of push-pull. The friction between them created heat, intoxicating and dangerous. But neither partner wanted to be consumed by it. That was the risk. To lose one's power, to be overtaken, to be burned.

Brooke was not used to taking orders, yet deep within her, buried beneath layers of control, that fantasy simmered. What she craved, at her most primal level, was strength. A demonstration of strength. Not the kind found in muscles or bravado, but in the unshakable force of a man who could withstand her. That was why she had tested David so often, probing for weaknesses, for cracks. If he could withstand her, if he could accept the full weight of her presence without shrinking, without running, then she could finally unleash all of herself.

But what test could she conduct in this environment? Was David simply barking orders or was he genuinely attracted - then, she looked. His lap. David was already excited. Fiercely so. The evidence pressed against his slacks, undeniable. She hadn't moved a single muscle and already she had his full attention. *Check,* she mused. Could she make it checkmate?

A slow surge of power pulsed through her, igniting deep in her core. She was not just craving dominance. She was craving a forum to wield her own power, a place and partner where she could feel that power radiate through her without resistance.

He wants a show, she thought, her lips curling into a wicked smirk. *I'll give him a show. Let's see if the leather-chair-boy can keep up.* Her purse hit the hardwood with a soft thud, her coat parachuting over it. Then, with the ease of someone reclaiming her throne, Brooke began to move, a slow sway of her hips.

Simple at first. Unhurried. Letting the rhythm settle into her body, letting it dictate the pace. Her movements built naturally, a teasing pulse side to side before evolving into a figure eight. She dipped lower, her body folding effortlessly into the motion, her backside hovering just above the floor - a feat in heels for sure.

She leaned forward just enough, arching her back, allowing a tempting glimpse of cleavage to catch the dim light. Oh, she knew this dance. It had been a while, but the terrain was familiar, and she maneuvered through like a seasoned traveler. Then, a deliberate shift. One leg stretched outward as her fingertips glided from heel to thigh, pulling her skirt up just enough to reveal a flicker of silk beneath.

David shifted in his chair. Not out of discomfort. Not out of restraint. But in that deliberate, dominant way that told her he was not unraveling - yet. But she knew she was breaking through. Her self-doubt had left the party long ago.

With all this power coursing through her, a new temptation arose. She wanted one last trial with him, pushing his limits by tasting him. *I kinda wanna gauge his hardness*, she thought, knowing that her lips would serve as the perfect barometer. The thought sent a hot pulse between her thighs, but she reined it in. No. That would surrender the game too soon. Tease him. No touching. She directed the show. Not him. Could he keep up?

Casually, she stood, turning away from him. As she did, her skirt lifted ever so slightly, just enough for him to glimpse the lace framing her backside. *That'll flip his limelight on.* She thought. Against the far wall, she spotted the loveseat - the perfect counterpart to his leather chair. A matching throne.

Brooke wandered toward the luxurious Chesterfield with a slow, practiced sashay that carried the composure of a runway queen. *Eat your heart out, Beyoncé,* her confidence purred. As she reached the seat, her arms guided her down with effortless grace. She did not sit - she descended, her curves floating like a feather before sinking into the leather's warm embrace. One leg crossed smoothly over the other, allowing just the faintest flicker of lace and silk to tease beneath the hem of her dress.

The ice in David's glass *clanked* as he took another sip, a subtle tremor betraying the effort required to keep his grip steady. Brooke tilted her head, stealing a glance. Ohhhh. His arousal strained against his slacks, thick and unyielding, his restraint barely holding. The sight sent a wave of satisfaction through her, feeding the fire already burning in her veins. She had him. And she was nowhere near finished.

He wants a show? A slow, sultry smile curled at the edges of her lips. *He'll never see one like this.* She wasn't about capturing a man. This was about something far greater. Brooke did not want to be *a fun date*, or even *a girlfriend.* No, she wanted something much more. Brooke wanted to be a memory. The kind that sears itself into a man's psyche, carving her name into the walls of his mind. She wanted to be the moment that came unbidden when he heard words like *seductive, alluring,* or better yet, *enchanting.*

If she finished herself off in front of him, she knew that he would never shake her from his thoughts. That sauciness would magnetically captivate him, sealing a piece of herself within his psyche. *Put this in your spank bank,* she mused, her confidence smirking at the idea.

Slowly, she let her body melt into the sofa, her frame slouching with sensual ease. Her legs uncoiled, stretching out as if claiming the space around her. Her fingers drifted beneath her dress as she arched her back.

And then - *clink, clink, clink.* The ice cubes in David's nightcap trembled against their glass prison like the first tremors of an impending earthquake.

Brooke's grin turned saucy. She was shattering his composure...just as he requested.

~ ~ ~ ~ ~ ~ ~ ~ ~ ~ ~ ~ ~ ~ ~ ~ ~ ~ ~

One by one, her manicured fingertips slipped open each snap of her blouse, moving with practiced precision. The delicate lace of her bra followed, the center clasp surrendering effortlessly to those same fingertips. Both garments slid away as if in unison, cascading down her skin. The heat from the room, mingled with the remnants of her rhythmic exertions, wrapped around her body, leaving a soft sheen on her breasts - a seductive glow she considered "a happy, sweaty accident." Her fingers traced a slow, deliberate path down her abdomen, riding the current of her body's subtle undulations. From the curve of her hip, her palm glided down the length of her outer thigh, paused with a graceful turn at her knee, and then wandered up her inner thigh in a lingering caress. Her back arched naturally, her breath unlocking as her hand made its return journey.

Brooke's gaze locked onto David's, her eyes burning with silent invitation. His composure was steady, but she saw the storm within him - an unspoken hunger. As her fingers teased their way inward, her eyes drifted upward, chasing the line of her arched spine toward the ceiling. In that moment, Brooke's inner enchantress was fully unleashed, and there was no taking her back.

Her fingers dipped teasingly beneath the lace of her matching panties, discovering just how wet she had become. The sensation was almost overwhelming, a delicious kind of embarrassment. She slipped the fabric to the side, enough that David could see her glistening, which is exactly the image she was going for. Her middle finger grazed the sensitive peak of her clit, and the pleasure washed over her in a slow, luxurious wave. She invited her index finger to join, the two digits framing her sweet spot like devoted bodyguards, creating a tension that was both protective and indulgent.

A soft, genuine moan sliced through the air, breaking the silence and signaling that this was no longer a performance, but something much more personal. What began as a power move had evolved into raw need. She craved the release in this manner. She panted, caught in the throes of her own game, her body walking the tightrope between dominance and surrender. Power aroused her, but something about the balance of giving in pulled her deeper.

Her lips parted as she gasped, eyes fluttering closed. *I still want him,* she thought, her mind spinning. Another gasp stuttered through her lips. *In my mouth.* But the stretch from the leather love seat to David's chair was too great. The trip would sober the intoxicating moment, and Brook was too feverish to make the trek.

Her fingers moved faster, circling her clit with increasing urgency. Another moan escaped her, this one raw, like the burn of a flame spreading across her skin. *I'm getting too close, too soon,* she warned herself, her fingertips relentless in their rhythm. Her vision blurred as she closed her eyes again, the world around her reduced to hazy shadows and glowing warmth. David was nothing more than a silhouette in the dim light, a shadow blurred by the veil of her own pleasure. Her velvet lips were fully exposed, open and vulnerable, her body arched and straining for more. She needed him. The thought hit her like a spark igniting dry leaves, she wanted him inside her.

When she opened her eyes, her breath caught in her throat. *He's gone!* Her gaze darted to the empty chair, confusion slowing the pace of her fingers for only a second. *Wait...* A sly smile curled on her lips when she spotted him. Through the haze of her growing desire, she saw him - David, standing directly above her. He had made the long journey across the living room to her, closing the space between them just when she needed him most.

She moaned again - a sound of surrender, pure and unfiltered. As David's fingers intertwined with hers, she yielded without hesitation, letting him take control. The warmth of his touch set her nerves ablaze, and her excitement surged. Brooke's fingers drifted upward, tracing the contours of his jaw, the line of his cheekbones, as though memorizing the face of the man who held her pleasure in his hands. Their eyes stayed locked, exchanging something unspoken, something electric. She knew her body would not last much longer under his spell.

David's touch was stronger than hers, but it carried her softness, as if he were preserving the very essence of her desire. His fingers circled her clit with calculated precision, swirling around her and never directly pressing her. If her clit were a city, David understood instinctively that the heart of passion thrived on the outskirts of town. Occasionally, one of his fingers would glide too close, skimming the sensitive center, sending a jolt of pleasure coursing through her. But he never lingered. He teased her with expert restraint, keeping her on the edge, building her higher. Brooke gasped, her breath stuttering in rhythm with his wet strokes, and bathing David's fingers in her erotic vintage.

Brooke's breathing quickened, her body arching as she neared the breaking point. She was lining up her final approach, each sensation coiling tighter inside her, ready to snap. But then, his voice, low and commanding, pierced the haze.

"You can't cum yet," he murmured.

Her eyes shot open, wide with desperation. "What?!" she begged, her breath ragged. "I'm so close... so *close*."

But David wasn't done. He leaned in, his fingers never slowing as they performed their intricate dance. His demand was firm, laced with just enough tenderness to make her ache. "You can't cum yet," he repeated, his tone deliciously cruel, "unless I'm in your mouth."

As if to punctuate his words, his fingers swirled in a sudden burst of acrobatics, pulling a shuddering gasp from her lips. Brooke's back arched, her body trembling with the effort of holding back. Her mind blurred, caught between the hunger to finish and the thrill of his control. She exhaled, a broken sound of longing, and conceded her position. She would obey. She had no choice, her body belonged to him now.

"Yes!" she moaned, her voice breaking like a desperate prayer. This balance of power was exactly what she needed.

"Oh my god," she scrambled, her fingers fumbling as she worked to unbuckle him. Her mind raced. *I'm not going to make it.*

But David's fingers never relented. They kept swirling, their movements steady and controlled as he gritted his teeth and repeated, calm but commanding, "My cock...needs to be...in your mouth...while you're cumming."

His fingers were Mozart, composing a masterpiece against her skin. A virtuoso. He knew exactly when to glide, when to press, when to tease. His touch played her body like a delicate instrument, weaving sensations she had never known existed. Each stroke, each caress, built into a crescendo as her back arched, her breath quick and uneven.

But she needed him, all of him. Her fingers frantically worked like she was searching for car keys in a horror movie, desperate and fumbling. *That damn belt*, she thought, cursing the obstacle. The leather snapped through the loops with a sharp whip of sound. "Oh my god," she gasped again, her toes curling over the edge of her climax as his fingers continued their intoxicating rhythm. His touch had shifted from melody to full-blown symphony, an orchestra of sensation that overwhelmed her senses.

Unsnap the slacks, she thought, as her hands moved with growing urgency. His fingers brushed her clit again, sending a shockwave through her. *Unzip the zipper.* The sound was deafening in her mind, like cymbals crashing in perfect harmony. His fingers plunged inside her once more, filling her, fucking her. The pounding of bass drums matched the pounding of her heart.

She was barely holding on. Her release built within her, an unstoppable force ready to break free. She teetered on the edge, her toes gripping the floor as she fought for balance. Her breath faltered for a beat. *Will I make it?* Almost panicking, she reached into his trousers, her fingers searching, desperate to find him. Another thrust of his fingers, another surge of pleasure. Trumpets blared in her mind.

There! Her fingers wrapped around him, freeing him from the confines of his slacks. The string section of her symphony swelled as her lips enveloped him, her tongue sliding along his length, drawing him deeper, assuring that she had crossed the threshold.

David thrust gently, his control unwavering, and she released a muffled moan around him. That final, tender push shattered her restraint. The fall began slowly, like the moment before a wave crashes, before the undertow pulls you under. She wrapped her legs tightly around his forearm, holding him there, needing him to stay connected as her body convulsed. Her pussy tightened around his fingers, pulsing in time with the rapid fluttering of her heart.

As Brooke's climax hit, her pussy pulsed with rhythmic intensity, sending shockwaves rippling through her body in two opposing directions. One wave surged upward, traveling along her abdomen, caressing her breasts, and swirling like a warm current around her neck before fogging her mind in a blissful haze. The other wave cascaded downward, wrapping around her thighs, making her legs tremble as it spilled into the arches of her feet and spread to the very tips of her toes. Shudder after shudder rolled through her, each pulse a mixture of uncontrollable spasms and electrifying pleasure. Her leg kicked instinctively, her back arching further, desperate for every last millimeter of his fingers. Another swell built and crashed over her, leaving her gasping as though she were an inexperienced swimmer caught in a powerful, unrelenting tide.

Both sets of her lips, her mouth and her pussy, claimed him. Brooke had taken him into herself, fully and completely. David's fingers plunged deeper, her walls clenching around him in waves as her release consumed her. Her mouth mirrored the same rhythm, Brooke's tongue teasing as she moaned a muffled tone through the waves of her liberation. Her pussy milked his fingers, while her lips milked him. Completely engulfed by his masculinity, she felt David release, as well, and welcomed it. She was submerged in the waves shared between them, wanting nothing more than to continue swimming within those currents.

Her body trembled as the final notes of their symphony played out. Completely entwined, they collapsed into the aftermath, a haze of breathless satisfaction. Brooke's body shuddered, savoring the lingering heat of their union, and for a moment, the world outside ceased to exist.

The waves gradually subsided, their once-overwhelming force softening into soothing ripples. Her body relaxed, and the spasms slowed to gentle, lingering aftershocks. Brooke closed her eyes, floating in the warm waters of her afterglow, content to drift there for a moment longer. The warmth embraced her, tender and intoxicating. He was still inside her, in more ways than one - claiming her, possessing her. And she had surrendered completely, willingly, the way her body had craved. This sea of warmth had overtaken her, but it felt right. Perfect.

With a breathless gasp, she slowly pulled herself toward the surface, her chest rising as she inhaled deeply. Her breathing steadied, her pulse slowing as she blinked up at him. Her hand still held him firmly, but her lips had released him. Their eyes met, and for a moment, time seemed to hang suspended between them. Brooke smiled - soft, satisfied, and playful - as she gazed into David's eyes. In that smile, she acknowledged what neither had to say aloud: their power struggle had ended in a draw. But the real victory was shared. Together, they had reached the symphony's final note, their bodies entwined in a duet that neither would ever forget.

A giggle bubbled up from her lips, light and flirtatious, and she winked at him. In surrender, she had discovered a different kind of power, one just as intoxicating as dominance. There would be more battles to come, more skirmishes waiting on another day. But for now, she basked in this warm, euphoric peace, knowing their game was far from over.

Morgan never stops writing. But only a few are trusted to read everything. Join his inner circle at
www.*TheKnightOfRomance*.com

Shifting Gears

Forbidden. Heady. Smoldering, with an intensity that refuses to be contained. Seductive sweetness mirrors hesitation as Abigail assesses the way he moves. Then comes the heat. Desire eclipses reason. The finish is lingering and irreversible with a bittersweetness that walks the lines between biology and morality. This story tastes like sin and lingers like a secret.

Suggested Pairings

Wine: Priorat (Spain)

Cocktail: Long Island Iced Tea

Coffee: Dark Temptation Espresso

Zero Proof: Midnight Reckoning

Indulge Freely
Morgan Knight

Some pleasures are meant to be savored slowly.
The beverage recipes can be found at
www.*TheKnightOfRomance*.com

Abigail froze. Something unimaginable had just taken root in her subconscious. If you're expecting murder, you're reading the wrong story. This ain't the Hallmark Channel. Though I see how you got there.

Abigail's mind was locked in an internal and dramatic courtroom battle. Both sides of the case held compelling arguments. As judge and jury in the matter, she sat in silence, listening to her internal prosecutor of social consciousness grill the witness on the stand - Mother Nature.

She wished this were a real courtroom, though, rather than the one unfolding in her mind. At least the chair would be more comfortable than the stiff polypropylene seat she had claimed while waiting at Seaside Elite Auto Service.

The day had been hellish. A high-speed drive through East Hampton's rolling hills and winding curves had seemed like the perfect remedy, an escape from the crushing weight of the argument still lingering like a storm between Abigail and her husband. In starting her therapy run, she had swiped the keys to the McLaren, a car they both loved, though she drove it much more frequently than he.

Abigail suspected her husband enjoyed the social prestige the vehicle afforded him, while she appreciated the car's true purpose - speed and performance. But on a critical turn, too absorbed in her mental courtroom drama, she hit the brakes hard. The line severed, spurting brake fluid across the engine, a known issue with McLarens. Fortunately, she hadn't struck anything. Just a simple spin-out. No injuries, but one casualty. Her phone had not survived the collision with the passenger door.

Now, stranded over a hundred miles from home, at night, in a service station, the inevitable loomed. If you think you know where this is going, you're probably right.

Still fuming from the fight, she resisted the notions of responsibility urging her to call home and explain. Plus, she was still angry with him. She had already handled the situation. What was there to say? Before leaving for the night, the service station owner had called in a specialist, a young mechanic who worked on high-performance vehicles. Living in one of the wealthiest communities in America had its perks, including round-the-clock, concierge-like service from highly skilled craftsmen.

In the waiting room, the courtroom battle in her mind raged on. The prosecutor jotted down a damning question: *Why won't your husband get himself checked out?*

Abigail knew the problem was not her. When it comes to biology, women just know. From the first time a girl notices a cute boy in junior high to the moment her biological clock starts counting to various hours - *a woman just knows.* For many women, the word "biology" and "intuition" are practically synonyms.

But, for assurances, she had herself tested. All systems operational. Science was now backing her argument, not just intuition. The problem was *him*, and she was once again requesting that he get himself checked out, a repeated request that now served as an annoying road closure sign.

His excuses and arguments for not getting examined had aged so poorly that they might now need a walker to stand up in court. Abigail smirked as her internal prosecutor grilled him: "Is senior care available for your arguments, sir?" But these were the facts of the case, and they were quite undeniable. His ego and pride were preventing her from relishing in one of the most majestic aspects of life. If Abigail wanted a child, drastic times might actually call for... well, you know.

~ ~

"Yeah. The line was severed," the young mechanic announced as he stepped into the waiting room.

Abigail snapped out of her haze. "Huh?"

"Your brake line. Severed. McLaren recommends regular maintenance. I checked the service database. Looks like your husband may have let this one slide."

Her mood softened. She suddenly appreciated how late the young man was working to help her. "Thank you," she murmured.

"Give me another ten minutes. I'll have you set. The shop will take care of billing in the morning."

Again, she whispered, "Thank you."

As he turned back toward the garage, Abigail caught him stealing a glance at her legs. Her tennis skirt had inadvertently ridden up slightly higher on her thigh, as she sat. She tilted her head, intrigued. *What was that?*

He disappeared into the shop, and she stood, peering in after him, not just to check on the car, but to study *him*. Curious, she toyed with an idea. Yes, he was roughly her husband's height. She had already noted his deep blue eyes, matching both her's and her husband's. So, you know - that matched. His build, though, was different, more athletic. Abigail attributed this to his lean muscle, emphasized by the sheen of brake fluid on his forearms, revealing veins thick with exertion. He had clearly thrown on his overalls fresh out of the shower, his raven hair was still damp. *Yeah*, she thought. *Given the right conditions, this young man could easily pass for a younger version of her husband.*

She entertained the thought for a moment. Then, her internal prosecutor introduced another compelling argument. One that appealed to her rebellious streak. Her husband would be livid if she introduced "bad blood" into the family line. A petty, outdated concern, in her opinion. If anything, that was a bonus in the final settlement.

The trial in her head was reaching its dramatic conclusion. The accumulated evidence was far too rational to be non-convincing. Social and moral forces had filed suit against Mother Nature and Abigail's biological clock. The case had landed on the court of polite society's docket. But the suit would likely be dismissed. Mother Nature's a bitch and a ruthless attorney when it comes to natural law. She *always* wins, even against polite society.

Abigail extended a long, smooth leg, taking one deliberate step into the shop. The garage was silent aside from the low hum of overhead lights and the distant melody of a mechanic's ratchet singing like crickets. Simply thinking about seducing this young man was making her wet. She stepped deeper into the space, savoring the contrast between the mechanical grit surrounding her and her own femininity.

She released her ponytail, letting her hair fall loose as her walk morphed into a saunter. A lock tumbled into her cleavage, the sensation sending a slow burn through her. And with that, Abigail knew.

As I said - when it comes to biology, women just know. The judgment was in. The court ruling in favor of Mother Nature.

~~~~~~~~~~~~~~~~~~~~

Abigail approached the front of the supercar, casually tracing her fingers along the vehicle's sleek curves.

The young mechanic, shutting the rear engine panel, flinched from being startled. "Oh! Huh. Didn't see you there."

She did not reply. She simply continued tracing the car, her gaze flickering to the gap in his overalls. His glistening torso and defined abs were a billboard for lust. He swallowed hard as she approached.

"You're all set," he said with a tightened voice.

She was close enough to feel the heat radiating off him. Leaning in, she whispered, "Thank you." Her breath was a feather against his skin.

He dropped his gaze to the floor, like a peasant before a queen. Abigail held her stare, waiting, allowing him the opportunity to summon himself. *Would he rise to her level?* Passion knows no class divide, but for passion to ignite, both people must see themselves as worthy. Abigail had acknowledged his merits. Would he see them within himself?

Tension crackled between them, hovering, suspended. She nearly turned away, until she caught him stealing another glance, this time at her
~~~~~~~~~~~~~~~~~~~~

ankles. His eyes trailed up her calf, along her thighs, over her hips, and around her waist. *Absorbing her.* Then higher, over her breasts, pausing at her shoulders before vaulting, directly, into her gaze.

Her smile warmed. Without a word, he had just complimented her.

All of us need someone who elevates us to the level of ourselves that we aspire to be. Abigail was able to serve as this elevator for the young mechanic with just her physical attributes. She suspected that he emotionally understood that phenomenon, but as a veteran, Abigail was able to process the sentiment at an intellectual level.

She leaned in again, this time pressing a wet-lipped kiss just below his ear.

"Thank you," she murmured.

Her hand slipped into his overalls, palm finding the hard ridges of his abdomen before descending lower, and her fingers audaciously seizing him. Her boldness startled the young mechanic as she brought her glistening lips to the corners of his mouth. Holding him within her palm, Abigail could feel him stiffening, rapidly. The socket wrench he had been holding clattered to the floor with a metallic curse.

He turned into her, pressing her against the McLaren with his hips and thighs. Her grip had unintentionally angled him downward. Through his overalls and her tennis skirt, she felt him, solid and urgent. His erection inadvertently stabbed her.

A sharp gasp escaped her. That sound, her breathless reaction, ignited something in him.

His hand swept down, finding the curve of her backside with unrelenting purpose. Years of gripping steel had honed his fingers into instruments of raw power, unyielding and commanding. When he seized her, the force of his shifting stole the breath from her lips, another sharp gasp breaking free before she could stop it. The strength in his grip was not just physical; but something deeper, something primal. She melted into that power, into him, savoring the unapologetic virility standing before her. Beyond these walls, social classes dictated order, rearranging themselves in rigid hierarchies, but here, within the charged circle of this garage, none of that mattered. Here, she was vulnerable, utterly, willingly - exactly where she wanted to be.

His lips moved in perfect harmony with hers, firm and insistent as he pulled her presence deeper into him. Her backside remained pinned against the cool metal of the car, a contrast to the heat building between them. His towering frame allowed his full lips to travel effortlessly along the curve of her jaw, drifting past her ear before descending onto the delicate slope of her neck. When his tongue traced a slow, damp path across her skin, a shiver coursed through her - nervous heat pooling at her upper lip, while a far more urgent warmth gathered lower.

Abigail's arms slid around his broad shoulders. Her fingers traced the thick straps of his workman's overalls, feeling the sturdy fabric which barely contained the strength beneath them. Then, without warning, he lifted her. His hands firm at her backside, hoisting her with effortless control. Instinctively, she wrapped her legs around him, her body molding to his. The solid wall of his chest met the softness of her curves. Her breasts absorbed the full force of his desire, an impression leaving no doubt as to how much he wanted her.

Their kisses deepened. Their bodies moved in perfect rhythm. Friction built with each clothed thrust. Abigail remained suspended in his arms, her weight nothing to him, his grip unwavering. In one fluid motion, he lowered her against himself, just enough for her to feel the full length of his erectness, before swooping her back up, resetting their position with effortless control. Their tongues mirrored the motion, thrusting into the heat of each other's mouths, lost in the heady interplay of lips and breath. Their respiration quickened, matching the pulse of their excitement.

Abigail gasped, her fingers scrambling for the buckles of his overalls, the cool metal pressing against the hard slope of his shoulders. Like a child unwrapping a long-awaited gift, she squeezed, releasing the clasps. The straps snapped free, whipping behind him as the heavy fabric slid down his waist, revealing the sculpted terrain of his back.

She reached for him instantly, fingers splaying over the ridges of his lats, nails digging into the firm muscle. The sharp sensation made him arch, his breath catching. Instinct took over. He pulled her closer, harder, until their bodies molded together in perfect alignment. Social constructs had long since melted away; this was something raw, something primal. Something endorsed by Mother Nature.

One of his hands drifted beneath Abigail's blouse while the other remained locked around her, keeping her pressed against him. His fingertips traced the edge of her sports bra, following the contour where supple skin met taut elastic. She knew he was teasing himself, savoring the moment, prolonging the inevitable. That slow, deliberate reverence awakened something deep within her - an element of her femininity that lay dormant for too long and now surged to the surface.

Restraint gave way to hunger as his hand slid beneath the fabric, seizing her with unspoken urgency. Abigail moaned, her body arching into his touch. His wrist and forearm flexed, pushing the bra upward in a single, forceful motion. The garment surrendered with a snap, its elastic retreating as his hands claimed what had been concealed.

Abigail's eyes flickered downward, drawn instinctively to the rigid proof of his desire. Her gaze traced upward, traveling over the ridges of his sculpted abdomen, each ripple accentuated by the dim light. The sight sent a jolt of excitement racing through her, a heat that coiled deep in her core. It was then that she noticed her own bare skin, the cool air kissing the exposed curves of her breasts. The realization sent another surge through her, an appreciation blooming in the moment.

Beneath her, a 710-horsepower engine rested within a precision-crafted frame, built for unrelenting performance. But standing between the sheen of her smoothly shaven legs was another work of art, one just as powerful, just as finely engineered, sculpted by labor and passion rather than metal and machines.

Her eyes lifted, meeting his, and she was struck again by his title: *Master Mechanic.* The words turned over in her mind, demanding a new definition: *one whose touch awakens the drive within highly sensitive, complex machines.* Her pulse skyrocketed, redlining in response. And when she found that same passion reflected in his unwavering gaze, when she realized she had become his most coveted machine, her entire body clenched with need.

She arched against him, accepting his unspoken compliment in the only way that felt right, by pulling his lips back to hers, melting into the rhythm of their mouths, tongues twining in a dance of reckless abandon. Then, against his lips, she whispered her verbal acceptance. "Thank you."

His lips left hers only to return to the delicate curve of her neck, trailing heat in their wake. He grasped the fullness of her rear, lifting her effortlessly to the edge of the car. His length slid against her, a teasing graze over her still-concealed heat, sending a pulse of electricity through her.

Abigail's lashes fluttered as she dared a glance downward through the intoxicating haze of their passion. She saw the weight of him, full and pulsing, teasing both of them with every deliberate thrust against her. Each time her body welcomed him, he stiffened even further, the sheer pleasure causing him to pulse against her again, as if shifting through higher gears.

Their eyes locked again, a silent exchange of hunger and understanding. Then, his hand landed between her thighs.

The moment his fingers met her, the thin fabric shrouding her pussy was gone, ripped away in an instant and discarded like a useless barrier between them. The rush of exposure sent a fresh wave of arousal crashing through her. Completely wet.

His cock landed against her again, and this time, there was nothing between them. Abigail exhaled sharply, a soft, breathy moan escaping as she glanced down once more, lost in the erotic splendor of it. His head throbbed against her, the smooth heat of her now-bare pussy coaxing him forward, inviting him inside of her.

Each slow, teasing pass of his length against her sent electric pulses through Abigail's body, his tip rumbling over her swollen clit, igniting her with every deliberate stroke. She moaned into the humid space between them, her breath catching with each slick glide. If he kept at this exquisite torment, she knew she could unravel right here, undone by nothing more than the sheer friction of his teasing restraint.

But then, he shifted.

The tantalizing grind was suddenly replaced by a slow, unyielding pressure, a deep, stretching ache that stole her breath and sent a sharp gasp from her lips. Her fingers flew to his shoulders, nails biting into his heated skin for steadiness. *He was inside her.*

Fully.

The power of him radiated through her, reverberating with a force that echoed upward, sending a wicked, twisting pleasure through her core. Her wetness welcomed him, granting him the ease to bury himself deep, *God he was deep*, until she needed a moment to fully absorb the sheer size of him. He paused there, still and solid within her, giving her body the space to yield, to adjust, to take him in completely.

As she did, a shiver fluttered through her, the involuntary quiver of her walls around him making his breath stutter. The effect was immediate, he withdrew slightly, only to thrust back into her, slow and deliberate, his cock stretching her in ways that made her tremble. Her body surrendered, melting into the rhythm as she leaned back, letting herself be *taken*. Any remaining restraint was now shattered.

His pace quickened, deepened, and Abigail felt the elegant supercar beneath them subtly rock in time with their growing, desperate rhythm. Just moments ago, she had struggled to take all of him, but now, she arched beneath him, demanding more, pleading for him with the tilt of her hips.

She was there, teetering on the edge, but she knew she had to hold back. *He must go first.* She thought. She needed him to. By going second, she knew that her body would uptake more of him within her. She needed to milk every last drop of him. But the strain of restraint was torturous. She could hear it in his breath, see it in the tightening of his jaw, feel it in the way he plunged into her with mounting urgency. He was near. How did she know? Again, *a woman just knows.*

He pulled back, and Abigail's gaze dropped, her breath catching at the sight of his length, completely coated in her arousal. The wet sheen of her own desire sent a fresh wave of heat through her. God, she was soaked for him.

She clenched around him instinctively, her body betraying her, begging him. A sharp groan rumbled from his throat. The sound alone nearly unraveled her. They moved in unison now, a perfectly calibrated machine, thrust for thrust, hunger for hunger. And when he drove even deeper, so deep she wondered if she had ever been taken like this before, she gasped in wonderment, throwing down the last of her resistance.

All night, she had only spoken one repeated phrase to him: "Thank you."

But now, she abandoned gratitude for something else. Something primal. Something desperate.

She leaned into him, her lips grazing his ear, her voice a breathy plea. A command.

"Cum inside me. Cum inside me. Cum inside me."

And then, to seal her demand, she wrapped her long, smooth legs around him, locking him in place, ensuring her request was met.

The moment the words left her lips, she felt the shift inside him, his entire body shuddering, his breath stalling, his muscles tightening. She had ignited something uncontrollable in him, something raw. He faltered, his balance wavering, drunk off her, lost in her.

Abigail braced herself and tightened her hold around him, just as he broke, feeling the depth of his penetration. A shudder wracked through his frame as he spilled into her. She felt him, his heat, the deep pulse of him as he emptied himself inside of her. The sensation sent fire through her limbs. His hips jerked, instinct driving him deeper, pushing his release further into her, coating her cylinder walls. And just when she thought it was over, just as her mind reeled from the sheer pleasure of it, he thrust again, growling low in his throat as another wave overtook him. Another release.

That was all she needed.

Her own climax seized her, crashing over her in wild, rolling waves. She cried out, the sound ripped from somewhere deep within. Her tone was one she'd only heard once before. Years ago, as a teenager, flying over a bumpy road, adrenaline coursing through her while nearly avoiding an accident.

She kept her legs locked around him, anchoring him inside as her body clenched and pulsed, drawing every last bit of his pleasure into her. Together, they rode out the madness, the chaos, the redlining of their shared ecstasy.

And then, slowly, they hit the clutch.

The rhythm of their bodies slowed, their frantic gasps softened, the world gently downshifted around them. Abigail swore she could hear the fading hum of an engine, the crunch of tiny pebbles beneath tires, the sound of a machine, once at its peak, now pulling onto the roadside.

He remained inside her, their bodies fused together in the aftershocks of what had just unraveled between them. Their breath came in staggered waves, rising and falling in unison, their heaving chests mimicking the steady idle of the engine beneath her. Neither moved. Neither spoke. They simply existed in that moment, bound and welded together by more than just touch. Without words, they understood. What had passed between them was not just physical, but something deeper, something unspoken yet undeniable.

Abigail softened their descent back into reality with slow, tender kisses just below his ear, her lips a whisper against his sweat-dampened skin. Still, she refused to let go. Her legs remained locked around his torso, holding him inside her like a padlock securing something precious. This was deliberate, an instinctive safeguard, her own silent plea to stay like this just a little longer.

She understood something fundamental. The longer he remained within her, the greater the chance that nature would take root. And, whatever great race had just begun deep within her, Abigail wanted to ensure there was a finish.

Finally, he adjusted, and she freed him - but slowly and deliberately, savoring every second. A silent grin passed between them as they pieced themselves back together, their movements unhurried, like dancers reluctant to leave the stage. As they dressed, shy and playful glances volleyed between them, teasing at the edges of something unspoken. When they finally surfaced from their moment, the young man shifted uneasily, his hands searching for something to anchor himself. He shrugged; his voice uncertain, almost dazed.

"I...I don't know what to... I don't know what came over me. I..."

Abigail hushed him with nothing but a look. Her eyes were full of a secret, knowing warmth. Without any hesitation, she pressed her lips to his, silencing his uncertainty in the gentlest of ways. Her hand slid down, disappearing into his overalls again, finding him still firm, still waiting. She squeezed, drawing in close to his ear, and whispered a final, breathy, "Thank you."

The world had softened, the edges of reality blurred like an impressionist painting. Everything seemed gentler - dreamlike, the glow of the garage lights, the cool kiss of night air on her skin. She pivoted around him with quiet grace. The car door clicked open with a hushed invitation.

She climbed in. The vertical door eased shut. The driver's side window rolled down with the faintest sigh. Even the engine, when it sparked to life, rumbled with an oddly subdued contentment, as if the machine itself had been lulled into a sense of peace. As the garage door lifted and she pulled away, even the stones beneath her tires seemed to snap in whispers, like crickets hushed by the weight of a secret.

The long drive home stretched before her; a ribbon of open road draped in moonlight. Abigail welcomed it. Hours alone, uninterrupted, to replay the night in her mind. Not once did regret stir within her. Instead, warmth spread through her chest - a gladness, pure and unfiltered. The young mechanic had been unexpected, yet perfect in his way. If she were his age, she could have easily imagined herself tangled in something reckless and beautiful with him, infuriating her father, delighting the rebel in her with her new mechanic boyfriend.

As she neared town, she bypassed the familiar turn home and instead veered toward the beach. The eastern sky blushed pink, the first quiet confession of dawn. The parking lot, empty and vast, welcomed her solitude. She silenced the car's engine. The supercar, always eager to flaunt his power, now reluctantly fell into silence.

Grabbing a cardigan from the passenger seat, she stepped out into the quiet.

The only movement came from the waves, rolling in tirelessly, their ceaseless work humming like an old song. Wrapping herself within the hug of the cardigan, she perched on the wooden fence rail, gazing out at the vast, restless sea. The fabric trapped her warmth, but it did nothing for the loneliness that stirred in the predawn hush.

Then, something changed.

The sensation began as a flicker in her abdomen, small, radiant pulses unfurling outward, in sync with the crashing tide. With each wave, a little more of the loneliness was swept away, as though the ocean itself was slowly washing away her loneliness. The last wave swelled within her, carrying something deeper, something wordless.

Suddenly, the sun crest - sunrise.

Golden light spilled across the horizon, wrapping her in an embrace. Abigail inhaled, her chest rising with the tide, her body alive with knowledge. She knew. Her plan had worked. How? That was the mystery of instinct. As I said, when it comes to biology, *a woman just knows*.

A single tear welled, unshed but glistening in gratitude. She turned her face toward the sun and the sea and whispered to those majestic forces, "Thank you."

Turn one last page - not in this book, but in your inbox. Morgan's next tale is waiting. Subscribe now for updates at www.*TheKnightOfRomance*.com

The Gravity Of Her Gaze

A classic vintage tale, with a lovely unique twist. This story whispers masculinity throughout its many layers. Irresistible pulls of darkness, cling to the edges as secrets unravel to a love far too intense to contain. The threat of love lost lingers with this smoky tale of lustful aches. Exceptionally complex, and perhaps like the rarest of vintages, this tale only deepens with time.

Suggested Pairings

Wine: Château Lafite Rothschild

Cocktail: Smoky Old Fashioned

Coffee: Espresso Romano

Zero Proof: Black Cherry Italian Soda

Should you wish to sip along with
the characters, these beverage recipes await at
www.*TheKnightOfRomance*.com

"Just tell me," Erin demanded, her voice sharp. I raised an eyebrow and teased, "Oh, now *that's* a convincing argument. I think it was the word 'just' that really sold me."

She slugged my upper arm. "Just...you know what I mean!"

"I do," I replied with a teasing grin.

She paused, pulling out an old reporter's trick that was something like 'good cop, bad cop', except in this case, Erin was both cops. She had been trying for ages to get me to spill personal secrets, something juicy she could sell to TMZ or Entertainment Tonight. But I was a vault, an impenetrable lock that only frustrated her ego, unable to crack my combination.

"Would you tell *me?* Just *me?*" she asked, leaning in.

"Off the record?" I confirmed, raising an eyebrow.

She nodded. "Yes."

I gave a dramatic pause, then smiled. "Perhaps."

I'd known Erin for years. She was an ambitious entertainment reporter, probably 20 years younger than me, but she had a fire that could not be ignored. What I respected most about her was how she refused to let her figure, or the lack thereof, debilitate her ambition. This is Hollywood. The city of angels is tough on women, especially women with fuller bodies. Hollywood's brutal, dismissive even.

The hill that Erin was climbing seemed impossible. A reporter. On-camera. How could she sell it? But against the odds, she was doing so. Her candidness, honesty, and infectious sense of fun had earned her millions of on-air interviews with celebrities, writers, and athletes. Over the years, we'd developed a strong trust. I was her first on-air interview, and we'd had several more since that time. Over the years, watching her saunter through the fusses and skepticisms launched by the less talented, I could not help but feel a deep sense of pride.

Her crew was packing up at a distance as I packed my briefcase. Erin leaned over the table, throwing darts of personal questions, praying for one of them to land some points. "Ever had someone you lusted after? Ever had a crush? Ever been in love?"

I let her darts land, replying, "Kid, I've had all of those. With the same woman. Simultaneously." Erin's jaw dropped. Bullseye.

~~~~~~~~~~~~~~~~~

As her crew continued loading their media van, Erin and I slipped into a booth at the Formosa Cafe, just a few blocks away. "This place is a joint," she chirped.

"Exactly," I confirmed.

Once we settled in and the waitress took our drink orders, Erin's curiosity came alive. "Tell me," she said, her eyes wide with anticipation. Her eagerness told me that this was a woman searching for hope. Maybe a token. A sign that she could point to when things got rough in any future romantic relationship. A story that might serve as a temporary anchor in her search and dealings with prince charming.

I did not sugarcoat things. "This story's a sample. A sample of life. It is *NOT* a fairytale. This is *my* story." I needed her to understand the terms and conditions of this contract, and to emotionally sign it with respect before proceeding. Hollywood is jammed packed with falsehoods. Most are glued together with fragments of cracked hope and fractured dreams that are packaged and sold to the public. This story, though, was like a fine liquor - to be shared between friends and for consumption purposes only.

Erin paused to absorb my words. Her sharp mind and intuition kicked in. The waitress quietly placed her Stoli and soda in front of her, and with a nod that spoke volumes, Erin replied, "I understand." And that's when I began.

~~~~~~~~~~~~~~~~~~~~

I was young. Younger than you. And she was even younger. Almost significantly so. But distance in age diminishes with passing years.

I'd had several female friends. There was never anything sexual about our arrangement. Well, maybe an occasional spark with one or two over the years. That interest flows both ways. It's inevitable. But for the most part, my circle was dominated by women. I like to think that's how I got into what I do. Years of coffees, dinners, parties, just socializing with women, led them to value my input on their relationship highs and lows.

That year, early June was sweltering. My friend Bella left a voicemail inviting me over for poolside cocktails with her, her husband, and the rest of our clan.

Erin interrupted, eyes narrowing. "Voicemail? She didn't text?"

"No", I snickered, "No texts back then, dear."

I hopped on my bike and rode several miles out to their place. I think I was testing myself, seeing how far I could pedal through the brutal heat. Everyone knew I was the odd duck in the group, and I was grateful they still accepted me. When I arrived, drenched in sweat and dramatically feigning the appearance of a desert refugee begging for water, I was met with warm laughter and claims like, "You're crazy".

I knew nearly everyone in our poolside parish, but I still meandered around the patio, offering my obligatory "hellos" and "good to see you's."

And then, I came upon *her.*

"Who?" Erin asked, intrigued.

I answered slowly, letting each letter land, my eyes locking onto Erin's. "*Her.*"

She was sunbathing. They say beauty hits men from several angles, and whether women admit this or not, most of them subconsciously subscribe to the theory. I could tell my words struck a personal chord of truth with

Erin. She wrapped her fingers around her vodka tonic and leaned in closer, eager for more.

Women may be more skilled at intuitively understanding attraction than men. Even for those who feel they hold absolutely no skills, again, there's at least an intuitive understanding of how it all works. But, few people - men and women - understand the source. Women will say things like "I need to lose weight around my butt or thighs," or "I should get bigger boobs." Whatever they feel is their physical deficiency when it comes to attracting a partner. These things may affect self-esteem, but they are NOT the true source of attraction.

Attraction emerges from attitude, arising from someone demonstrating that they're going to get a bang out of life, no matter what personal, physical, or financial obstacles they face. That's magnetic. We can't help but be drawn to that type of person. Because these attitudes are rare. That attitude is full of life. And, that which is full of life, attracts the energy to propagate life. The desire to propagate life, that's sexual attraction. Doesn't matter if you're male or female.

This projection of that attitude resides in only one part of the body. Do you know what it is?

Erin thought for a moment, then started guessing. "Muscle tone? The way they move? Their skin? How well a person takes care of themselves? Their walk? The MIND – her final answer."

I smirked. "Their eyes."

Erin nodded, her own eyes widening as she recognized the truth. "Ohhhh. Yeah."

That's why people describe eyes in so many ways: "Cautious eyes," or "her doe-like eyes," "green eyes," "wide eyes," "blue eyes," "bold eyes," "exquisite eyes," "handsome eyes," "fearful eyes," "stunning eyes." Whatever *energy* a person exudes is reflected in their eyes.

Erin leaned in, comprehending. She understood that what I was saying was not just an opinion but grounded in evolutionary psychology. I'd written about these phenomenon in several books and discussed the ideas in lectures over the years, but I had not directly addressed the idea with someone like Erin, who was petitioning me to continue.

Like I said, when I approached her, she was sunbathing. Her features were delicate, radiating femininity. Being from the old Soviet bloc, her milky skin yearned for a touch of sun, but her Polish genetics had other plans, no matter how much she tried to coax a tan. She'd slather on lotions and oils, but the sun gods were not listening. Adjusting her approach, she donned the perfect attire for sun worship over her hourglass figure: a jaw-dropping, baby-blue bikini. And, over the summer, her commitment to the art of "laying out" eventually yielded a hint of a sun-kissed glow.

Speaking of her figure, ever wonder why guitars also have the same hourglass shape as a woman? That's probably not an accident.

But, this woman's figure pulled attention as naturally as a flower's petals attract bees. In a word, she was *pretty*, though her sunglasses hid the road to her greatest asset. She was the last person I needed to greet in my rounds. I approached her, extended my hand as a polite gesture, and introduced myself. With equal grace, she mirrored my move, offering her fingertips in formal greeting while lifting her sunglasses with the other hand. "I'm Natalia," she said.

In lifting those sunglasses, that's when her eyes flared into my unconscious mind. What women often don't realize is that, in moments like these, men can fall into something close to an entrancement, being drawn in as if they're under a spell. Hell, the idea's so old the Egyptians and Greeks even wrote about them.

Her eyes were not merely *ocean blue*. No, they held the blue of *all* the oceans, all the seas, woven together into something vast and infinite. The kind of blue you'd see gazing at Earth from the heavens, where every tide, every secret depth, dissolves into a single, breathtaking expanse. And in the slight squint of her gaze, I read a message more vivid than words: *Not only am I going to get a bang out of life, but yours will never be the same.*

In moments like that, men feel two things, lust and fear. Oh, and we also feel stupid. If you ever see a man acting like an idiot, there's usually one of two reasons. First, and the most common, he really is *that* stupid. The second? He's just been affected by a woman's eyes.

My stupidity surfaced the moment she set a boundary. "You can stick your foot in the pool, but you can't go for a swim," she informed me.

Thinking I was clever, I tossed back, "You can feel the punishment, but you can't commit the sin." A joke. A nod to an old '80s tune from Howard Jones, *No One Is to Blame*, a song that, ironically, could have become our soundtrack. But my joke hit the ground like a lead balloon. No laugh. Not even a smirk.

Instead, she gave me a puzzled look before replying flatly, "No. You're all sweaty. That's gross. Swimming in someone's sweat?" She wrinkled her nose, then hesitated. Something shifted in her expression. A flicker of mischief. With a kittenish smile, she corrected herself with a teasing postscript. "Well, swimming in someone's sweat isn't *always* gross."

In that moment, even though the sky on that day was flawlessly clear, I will swear to you that I heard the distant rumble of thunder.

~ ~ ~ ~ ~ ~ ~ ~ ~ ~ ~ ~ ~ ~ ~ ~ ~ ~ ~ ~

Through delicate conversational probing, I learned that Natalia was staying with a mutual friend, Valerie, who was also at our poolside gathering. Natalia was not an exchange student; she had already completed her education. She was simply being hosted by Valerie and her husband while she considered making a permanent move to the States.

My friends quickly caught on that I was smitten. Subtlety had never been my strong suit. That's why I don't play poker. I suck at it. I was never very good at burying feelings. Erin smirked at my unintentional vulnerability, sipping her fresh Stoli and soda through a thin straw while politely motioning for me to continue.

The rest of the day was a battle between restraint and sheer fascination. My soul wrestled with the fine line between admiring Natalia and maintaining some semblance of social decorum. Any opening that arose where I could lock in a momentary gaze or talk to her without locking up the gears of social awkwardness, I seized it. Our conversations were playful, but being around her felt like trying to breathe at high altitude. I found myself slipping away to the kitchen more often than necessary, just to regain composure.

From the window, I stole glimpses of her, lingering longer than I should have. I felt ridiculous, like some lovesick fool, barely able to function. But, I needed time to breathe.

During one of these self-imposed kitchen retreats, Valerie, the one hosting Natalia for the summer, wandered in. I expected small talk, something about the heat or how good the pool felt. Instead, she caught me off guard with a single, measured warning.

"You can't have her."

I blinked. "What? Who?"

"Natalia, you dumbass." Valerie's voice was sharp, edged with something between frustration and anger. She doubled down, repeating herself. "You *can't* have her."

"Me?" I asked, feigning innocence. "What are you talking about?"

Valerie folded her arms. "EVERYBODY can see it." Then, with a calm but firm finality, she said, "Stay away."

A beat passed. Something shifted in her expression, like a thought had just struck her. Then she added, almost as an afterthought, "Besides, she's engaged."

The conversation was brief, but it landed like a sucker punch. Valerie turned toward the patio door just as desperation slipped into my voice. "And if I don't?"

She stopped, gripping the doorframe, then looked at me across the kitchen with unnerving certainty. "Then I'll send her back. She's only here for the summer anyway."

With that, she slipped outside, shutting the door behind her with quiet precision.

That entire interaction with Valerie was abnormal. Peculiar. I got the sense that Valerie wasn't just being territorial, she was protecting Natalia. But from what? I wasn't some womanizer with a reputation to defend. Hell, my younger self would have loved to be known as that kind of guy. But I wasn't. So why the warning?

And was Natalia really engaged? That bit of information felt contrived, like a hasty exclamation. Everybody else seemed cool with Natalia, me, and pretty much the entire crew. So, why was Valerie so damn angry?

The situation was a heaping mess. I now had a craving for a woman who generated so many butterflies within me that I could be an entomologist. That girl may, or may not, be engaged. She was only here for the summer. And, for some unknown reason, her hostess was hellbent on keeping me away. Quite the uphill trek when all I wanted was for that Polish beauty to fall in love with me.

My memory's a little hazy, but I'd say about a week had passed since I met Natalia. And damn if she hadn't stirred something deep inside me. Dreams. Intense dreams. In one, where we picnicked together. Seriously? Who the hell picnics anymore? Even back then, people weren't doing it. So why was I dreaming about one?

Natalia had set everything up, a perfect spread. She sat cross-legged in a flowing white cotton dress, a massive picnic basket beside her. She reached in, never breaking eye contact, and slowly pulled out one large can of peaches. She set them in front of me. Next, she handed me a can opener, flashed a coy smile, and said, "Enjoy."

"Put *that* in your Freudian pipe and smoke it.", I said.

Erin smirked. "This is right out of a film noir."

"Tell me about it," I replied.

~ ~ ~ ~ ~ ~ ~ ~ ~ ~ ~ ~ ~ ~ ~ ~ ~

Over the summer, three pivotal events happened. The first was at the local coffee shop. This was Small Town, USA, so there was only one coffee shop. I was sitting in one of the two matching wingback chairs, reading, completely absorbed, my book held high, blocking out the world. Then, I felt a gentle poke on my knee.

I lowered the book, and who do you think was sitting across from me?

"Natalia," Erin guessed.

"You got it."

She was leaning forward, elbows on her knees, absentmindedly chomping on her gum. She grinned and simply said, "Hi."

She was wearing black leather pants and a white tank top. Leather pants. In July. And somehow, she wasn't even sweating. The voltage radiating off this woman had more wattage than a rock star's stage lights. And damn if I wasn't addicted to the charge that she gave me.

"Whatcha readin'?" she asked.

"A b...ba...boo.." I needed a second to collect myself. "A book."

She nodded, completely unfazed by my awkwardness. "A book?" She smirked. Her confidence was unwavering. "That's good."

Right then, the barista called her name. Natalia popped up, gliding past me to grab her iced latte from the counter. As she headed for the door, she swung around, locked eyes with me, and said, "K, call me." Then, just like that, she disappeared into the sunlight, like a summer ghost.

"Call me?" My brain scrambled to process her words. Hadn't I just fumbled that interaction? I was sure I had failed. So, what was this *call me* bullshit?

I kicked myself for freezing up. At the same time, I was ecstatic. She'd told me to call her. Not asked, but told, which meant she was probably interested. Right? But I'd barely managed to string enough words together to qualify as a sentence during our conversation. I hadn't even talked to her, let alone gotten her number. And now, all I wanted was a second chance of our interaction. A do-over.

Erin interrupted, shaking her head. "This doesn't sound like the confident guy I know."

I exhaled. "I was young. Confidence takes time to grow, piece by piece. Failures and challenges like these are the manure that make confidence take root. Men hatch into our manhood, into our confidence. Bit by bit. Event by event. Women have a biological marker as to when they're beginning to enter adulthood. For men, no such marker exists. We used to hold rituals which would welcome a boy into manhood, but those rituals have pretty much died out."

I could see Erin holding a momentary, empathetic stare for the men in her life, nodding before she returned her attention to the story.

I tried to focus on my "b-b-b-book", forcing myself to lock in on just one paragraph at a time because I was swooning over the Natalia conversation. Then, I felt another poke on my knee. My heart leapt. A second chance. I peeled the book away from my face, grinning, only to find Valerie sitting across from me. Her expression was carved from stone, a scowl so severe it looked painted on, "Stay. Away." She turned her head toward the window and added a confident, "I *will* send her back, if..."

She never finished the sentence. She didn't have to. I knew exactly what she meant. But what Valerie did not understand was that staying away was becoming emotionally impossible.

~~~~~~~~~~~~~~~~~~~~

The second incident happened a few weeks later. Midsummer now. Natalia's time in town was running out. The pool party couple was hosting another event, this time for the wife's birthday. An evening affair with a bonfire, live music both inside and out, drinks, dancing - the works. Knowing how over the top these friends could get, there was probably a last-minute debate about hiring trapeze artists. You only turn thirty-nine once.

I arrived and made my usual rounds, weaving through the pasture of social cattle with the right amount of charm. But in truth? I was not there for the party. I was James friggin' Bond. On a mission. Find Natalia. And at the same time, skate the edge of Valerie's surveillance. Evade the eyes of her many legionnaires. Stay two steps ahead of her.

The place was packed. Loud. A pianist's fingers danced along the keys, spilling improvised jazz into the air. Then, I sensed her, Natalia was here. Not in a supernatural way. I could smell her perfume. The musician greeted me with a casual, "Hello", but my attention was elsewhere. I scanned the room for Valerie, tracking her like an enemy agent. Keep your enemies close, right?

I peered through the glow of a candelabra on the piano and into the crowded room beyond, when I saw what I'd been looking for. A woman tossing her hair. And when she turned, I instantly recognized the contours of her pretty face. If Natalia were Waldo, I could find her every damn time, on every damn page, probably in the damn dark, too.

She saw me and smiled. I swear she knew I had been searching for her. I started toward her, but two steps in, I stopped - cold. Natalia leaned slightly away as a man, some guy, placed a soft kiss on her cheek and handed her a champagne flute. But she never broke eye contact with me. Natalia had brought a date.
~~~~~~~~~~~~~~~~~~~~

"WHAT?!" Erin shouted. Heads in the pub turned, momentarily thrown by her outburst.

"I know," I said, shaking my head. "I was wrecked."

Erin sputtered, struggling to find the words. "How could she? What was she - ? I just don't under-"

"I know," I repeated. "I was in the same boat."

She leaned in, determined. "What did you do?"

Well, I couldn't have explained this at the moment, but something in Natalia's body language told me she wasn't really into this guy. The way she turned from his kiss. There was no affection. But I needed a week or so at that time to fully process what had happened.

Erin wasn't satisfied. "No. What did you do in *that* moment?"

After my brief hesitation, I pressed on, continuing my trajectory toward Natalia, without the slightest idea of what I'd say when I reached her. As I moved through the crowded room, Natalia's gaze dipped downward, as if weighed by guilt. Though she carried herself like a rock star, she was not heartless. She knew she had hurt me. She knew there was something cosmic between us - something neither of us had found the words to describe. And she knew she had just betrayed that celestial trust.

I was only a few paces away when, BAM. A woman stepped directly into my path, so suddenly and so close that my eyes needed a second to refocus.

"Noooo", Erin groaned, already predicting the interference, "Valerie?"

"Mhhhmmmmmm." I confirmed.

Valerie didn't waste any time. "A word?" Her voice was low, firm. Her breath was warm against my nose. Before I could react, she grabbed my arm and pulled me from the crowd. I let her. This was the only socially acceptable escape from the awkward moment I was about to encounter with Natalia.

She led me to a dimly lit hallway, away from the noise and the guests. The air changed. I felt like I was being summoned to the principal's office, and I was preparing to have my ass handed to me. Detention was almost certain. Expulsion? Possible. I was still trying to process the *Natalia-has-a-date* situation when Valerie cornered me.

Her signature scowl was sharper now, her eyes burning into me. She raised a perfectly manicured finger, sharp as a switchblade, and pressed it into my sternum with an accusatory force. She said nothing. Just stared, unblinking, into my curious gaze.

Then, with one swift motion, she glanced over her left shoulder, then her right, grabbed my collar, and kissed me.

"WHAT?!" Erin practically jumped out of her seat.

I leaned back, exhaling. "She kissed me."

"No, no. I heard you," Erin said, shaking her head in disbelief. "I just... I can't believe... she *really* kissed you? What the...?"

My lips detected traces of vodka and lemonade. My feet cemented themselves to the floor, and my body followed suit, stiff, frozen. Valerie kept pressing forward, trying to draw a reaction out of me. But no dice.

She doubled down, pressing her body and breasts against my chest, her hand slipping toward my groin. Again, no dice. Eventually, she gave up, resting her head against my chest with a long, heavy sigh. I could feel the steam escaping from whatever internal pressure she had been building. She started rocking me gently, side to side. I remained motionless. Inside and out.

Then, her voice came, muffled against my chest. "You want her, don't you?"

I swallowed and cleared my throat.

Valerie pulled away, exhaling sharply as she said, "Sorry. I will."

I frowned. "Will what?"

She met my eyes; her expression was hauntingly unreadable. "I will send her back. Being here is obviously torturing you too much."

She stepped into the light, then disappeared into the party. But just before she left, she turned, lifted her manicured, switchblade finger, and pointed between us. "Oh, and this?" She dragged the blade-like nail to her lips in a slow, deliberate "*shhhh*". Then, just like that, she dissolved into the crowd.

"This chick is *fuuuuuuuuuuuucked* up." Erin testified.

I chuckled and smirked in agreement with her, then let out a deep breath before continuing.

Emerging from the dim hallway, I felt like stepping out of a cave, blinking against the brightness of the party. Valerie was gone, blending somewhere into the sea of bodies. But neither my heart, nor my mind, was on her. Natalia. Where was Natalia? Had she seen us? I scanned the room, searching through the shifting ocean of partygoers. The crowd was a blur of swaying bodies, laughter, and the occasional "Wooo-hooo" from jello shot takers.

Nothing.

I asked a mutual friend if they'd seen Natalia. "She's gone.", they said. My shoulders dropped. Dejected, I made my way to the exit, weaving through the drunken currents of the house. On my way out, I passed by the swimming pool. And that's when I saw Valerie, yet again. She was in the pool, with her husband. Naked. He had her pressed against the pool ladder, their bodies tangled, moving. Other people swam around them, oblivious or simply not caring. She never saw me.

Erin shook her head, doubling down on her assessment, "Yeah, reeeeeeaaaaaallllllly fucked up."

That night was the longest of my life. I had no idea where Natalia was. No idea what she was doing. No idea who she might be doing it with. Sleep never came. Instead, I lay stretched out on my back porch, staring up at the stars, a cigar burning between my fingers.

And that's when a revelation hit me. Stars align themselves to one another based on predetermined forces. The energy and rules that govern their interactions came into being long before the stars even existed. Natalia and I resided under those same sets of stars and were therefore governed by those same laws, the same magnetic forces, of energy, and gravity. Just as planets are predestined to orbit one another in a specific pattern, so are we humans. We orbit one another, whether we realize this or not. And in my case with Natalia, I knew that I was within her orbit, and she was in mine. Our choices had nothing to do with the situation. Physics was in the driver's seat, and our emotions were simply along for the ride.

Erin let out a slow breath, almost a whisper of realization. "Holy crap." She turned her head away, absorbing the weight of the revelation.

What I also realized that night was that Valerie had been using me. Keeping me in reserve, a backup plan for whatever she needed. But I hadn't done anything about it. Yet! Like I said, men do not become men all at once. We hatch into becoming men, piece by piece, shaped by the challenges we confront. Valerie, and her threats, were one of those developmental challenges that I would have to face as part of my own hatching process.

I turned to Erin. She clutched her glass like a lifeline.

"Another?", I asked.

She fired back, "No." Then, more forcefully, "Don't stop."

Two weeks dragged by. No word from anyone. Radio silence. I found myself spending more time with another buddy, who was outside of the gang's preferred provider network. He and I were shooting pool at a country tavern one evening. Hell, it was almost a saloon, complete with grungy barstools, neon beer signs, and a stage showcasing local country crooners searching for their break.

Erin cut in. "Wait. You shoot pool?"

"Used to," I admitted. "Poorly."

Truth was, I just needed an excuse to get out of the house. We were knocking back cheap drinks with cue sticks in hand. We were surrounded by locals just like us, washing away their misery with piss-like beer. Then, like a gust of wind before a thunderstorm, the entrance door flew open.

Valerie, or whatever name she was going by that night, blew in first, all attitude and pre-autumn air. Natalia trailed in her wake. Her gaze found mine instantly. And just like that - gravity. A pull, deep and undeniable. Valerie noticed our glances. She smirked but said nothing.

The obligatory introductions to my buddy followed. Valerie, ever the orchestrator, suggested we join them. My buddy, always one to read a room, bowed out smoothly, flashing a charismatic smile as he gestured toward Valerie. "You two wouldn't mind giving this loser a lift home, would you? I was his ride."

Valerie did not miss a beat. "Of course, we will."

And that's when the night took a turn.

Erin scoffed. "Huh. Interesting."

I had already figured things out. Valerie was not there for a drink or to unwind like the rest of us. She was here to seduce.

Erin's eyes narrowed. "You?"

I shook my head. "No. Her target was the guitarist this time."

That was the final straw for Erin. She threw up her hands. "She's cheating on her husband? First you, well almost you, and now the guitarist? What is wrong with this woman?", she asked?

I didn't answer. I let Erin work through her story character outrage as I continued.

Before we even had time to settle, the guitarist descended on us, drawn to Valerie like a moth to a bug zapper. She giggled. He grinned. They were in their own little world, caught up in whatever game they were playing.

But across the table, Natalia and I existed in a universe of our own.

She reached out, gently taking my hand, turning my palm over in hers, studying the lines as if she could trace my past and read the choices that I had made. Her expression softened. Sorrow edged her eyes.

She whispered, "How come?"

I met her gaze. "How come, what?"

Natalia was not the effortless, magnetic rock star in that moment. She was something else. Something raw.

"You never asked me out," she said, her voice barely above a breath. "I waited all summer. You never called. You never..."

I cut her off, leaning in. "Valerie said she would send you back to Poland."

She blinked. "So?"

"So, I was screwed either way," I admitted. "You have no idea how much I've thought about you."

Natalia exhaled sharply, shaking her head. "I'm only here for six more days."

"I know."

Natalia looked agitated, like she needed to shake off the weight of the conversation clinging to her skin. She pushed back from the table, standing abruptly. Then, with a glance toward Valerie, she bent down and whispered into my ear, her breath warm, her words scorching.

"If she was going to send me back..." A pause. A shift. And then - a dagger to the heart. "I would've just stayed with you."

The floor tilted beneath me. Her lips brushed against my ear as she continued, her voice a breathy blade slicing through my chest, "Riding you each night. Waking up naked with you each morning. Not a bad way to spend a summer". She straightened, turned, and left me there, stunned, gutted, reeling.

I sat frozen, her words replaying on an endless loop in my mind. Kicking myself. If I had only known. *Goddamn!*

Before I could fully process the ache in my ribs, Valerie's new conquest leaped to his feet. The band was warming up, tuning their instruments, and running mic checks. He pulled Valerie in, devouring her mouth in a sloppy and disgusting, wet-tongued spectacle. He threw a smug glance in my direction and strutted off to the stage.

Valerie, practically vibrating with satisfaction, turned her attention to me. A slow, knowing grin spread across her lips. "Remember? If you -"

"FUCK YOU, Valerie." The words ripped from my throat like gunfire. The nearby tables went silent. My voice carried steel. Unshakable. Absolute.

"You think you can control people? Play games? Manipulate lives?" I leaned in, eyes locking onto hers like crosshairs. "Here's a warning for *you*, you seditious little cunt, if you so much as *think* about meddling in my romantic life again, your husband will know about all of your indiscretions. Your superiors will know. Our friends, your priest, the goddamn President of the United States will know. They will all know."

Valerie's smugness evaporated.

"I don't care what happens to me," I continued, voice low, lethal. "I don't care about your retaliation. I control the outcome of my life. Not you. Is that clear?"

She shrank. The predator had just been declawed.

I wasn't finished. "I asked you a question. Is...That...Clear?"

Her shoulders caved. Her poise crumbled. "Yes," she muttered, her voice revealing her true cowardness.

For full assurance that she would now respect me, I tilted my head. "Yes... what?"

She hesitated. "Yes...?"

I gifted her the answer. "Yes...Sir." I paused. "From now on, you can address me as 'Sir.' Is that also clear?"

She swallowed hard. The words barely escaped her lips. "Yes...Sir."

I didn't linger. I squared my shoulders, turned on my heel, and stormed out.

Six days. That's all I had before Natalia left. Maybe that was just enough time to align our orbits, to pull her back into my gravity field. Maybe it was enough time to convince her to stay.

Erin, wide-eyed, exhaled sharply, "Jesus Christ," she muttered. "This is good."

~~~~~~~~~~~~~~~~~~~~~~~~~

As I sat there with Erin, I faded, not out of rudeness, but because my mind was no longer in the present. The past had swallowed me whole. Like a high-definition dream, I relived the experience. Erin dissolved into the background, and the memory took center stage. That's the magic of tenderhearted moments, they play like films, written, directed, and produced by our unconscious, crafted solely for us.

The scent of whiskey clung to the air, thick as the swirling smoke. The barroom felt darker now, heavier, as the late-night hours settled in. Shadows stretched across the worn wooden floor. Conversations slurred. Laughter turned lazy.
~~~~~~~~~~~~~~~~~~~~~~~~~

Having hatched a little more into manhood, I was on the hunt for Natalia, scanning the room, my pulse drumming in my ears. She wasn't far. She had stepped outside, probably needing the sharp burn of a cigarette after the fiery relief of a shot to steady herself. Vulnerability without reciprocity can do that to a person, those emotions demand escape, if only for a moment.

She was strolling back into the tavern, one hand tucked into the pocket of her faded blue jeans, her gaze pinned to the floor. But the second she saw me, she stopped. The world narrowed. The entryway was empty, save for a lonely, busted piano shoved off to the side, the keys yellowed with time. Natalia didn't speak. Neither did I. That unspokenness surged between us, thick as the whiskey in the air.

Like a gust of raw intent, I closed the distance between us, fast and sure, leaving a wake of electric purpose behind me. Natalia barely had time to react before my hands found her pretty face, framing her cheeks as my lips crashed into hers.

She inhaled sharply, a split second of stillness, then surrendered.

As the force of my momentum caught up with us, I lifted her from the ground in one fluid motion, her firm buttocks settling against my forearms. Instinct took over, her legs wrapped around my waist, her fingers tangling in my hair as her mouth welcomed my tongue. I turned, sweeping her with me, pinning her against the wooden slat wall with enough force to knock the breath from both of us.

We gasped in unison.

The fever of our collision, lips, limbs, and desire, flushed through me, unraveling any remaining restraint I might have had left. I felt her react, the shift of her hips, the arch of her body pressing into me. I knew that she could feel me swelling against her, and I never faltered with embarrassment. I wanted her to feel me in that vulnerable state, confirmation of her effect on me. There was no shame, no hesitation. Whether it was validation she needed, I didn't care. I wanted to give her whatever she needed, and I needed to take her. I needed to unleash my virility, unapologetically. Just another stage, hatching into manhood.

My lips pulled back just enough to meet her gaze. Locked in. My vision recalibrated on those beautiful eyes before me. I thrusted against her, trapping Natalia between myself and the wall, and delivering a slow, deliberate confirmation of intent. Her body bowed, her feet never touching the floor, arms tightening around my neck for balance. Her eyes fluttered shut. And when they opened, those stunning blue irises found mine.

A breath. A tremor. Then, the slightest nod. A silent whisper of the only word I needed, "yes". I hoisted her higher, staggering back, scanning for cover, for somewhere, anywhere, to land. Six feet away, an open entryway caught my eye, a storage closet filled with broken tables and forgotten chairs. No door. Just a tired red curtain sagging from its rod, a flimsy pretense of privacy. On the other side of the closet wall was the band's stage. The drummer, two feet away, directly through the wall. But right now, nothing else existed. Nothing but her. I swept us inside, and as Natalia pulled the red curtain shut behind us, we disappeared, like a magician and his lovely assistant, vanishing from the world outside.

Our lips never lost contact, still locked in their fervent debate. I lowered her onto a broken chair, the wood creaking beneath her, but neither of us cared. Desperation wasn't the right word. Determination. That was it. Standing before her, I unzipped, my movements slow, deliberate. Natalia remained still, unmoving, unreadable. The tension in the air crackled like static before a storm.

Then, with a sudden, hungry impulse, I crushed my lips to hers again. One hand found her wrist, lifting her arm as if leading her into a dance. A twist. A spin. A controlled 180-degree pivot. Before the turn was fully completed, I halted her, my hands now resting firmly at the backside curve of her hips. From behind, I dipped my head to her neck, inhaling her, my lips finding that delicate hollow just below her ear. She reached back, fingers threading into my hair, her breath sharpening as I traced that sensitive spot with my tongue.

She felt my hardness against her, there was no mistaking it. The hard press of my desire against the curve of her denim-covered backside. My hand slid forward, palm grazing her stomach before slipping lower, disappearing beneath the waistband of her Levi's. And then, I found her. Softness unlike anything else. Full. Warm. Forbidden in its perfection. My fingertips bore witness to something sacred, something intoxicating. A moment of reverence before hunger overtook reason.

Natalia exhaled, her body pressing into my touch, her blue eyes dark with approval. I did not hesitate. My hands were quick, precise, no fumbling about. Her jeans were unfastened in an instant, her zipper gliding down. In one swift motion, denim slid to her knees and her panties following without protest. With firm resolve, I placed my palm between her shoulder blades. Natalia surrendered effortlessly, bending forward, her elbows bracing against a wooden bar stool.

She pressed back against me, her warmth drawing a deep, primal response from within. She felt me align with her, and I could feel the way she welcomed me. With a fistful of her hair, I pulled her just enough to claim her attention, then pressed forward.

She stood on her toes, taking me in, her breath catching as she absorbed the moment. I stayed there, savoring the way her body adjusted, the way her inhale caught before releasing in a shuddered exhale. Natalia leaned back, keeping me inside of her. Her movements were slow and unhurried. With deft fingers, she unfastened her blouse, peeling it open, exposing her sun-kissed skin to the dimly lit space. The sight of her stole my breath, but I had none to spare, I was already lost in her.

I moved again, slowly at first, and she pressed back against me in perfect response. Her arms lifted, wrapping around the back of my neck, drawing my mouth to hers. Our lips met in a heady collision, her gasps dissolving into my breath, her moans barely audible over the steady pound of the drummer on the other side of the wall. That song was ours alone.

Natalia melted against me, her body opening, drawing me deeper. My hands locked onto her hips, my grip tightening as I guided her into the rhythm of our own making. My movements turned more insistent, our connection driving forward like the relentless push of a locomotive on steel tracks. I wasn't fucking her. I was taking her. Claiming her. We were aligning our orbits together. The tempo built. Faster. Harder.

She clung to me, her breath coming in staggered gasps, her hair falling messily into her face as she surrendered to the motion, to the force of it all. Every shift, every pull, every thrust propelled us toward something inevitable, something unstoppable.

I felt her body beginning to shudder and seize up within my hands and forearms. Her muscle's ability to support her began to dissolve. She was a rag doll, and I completely supported her. She gasped. Stood on her toes, her spine arching as her boiler redlined. I held myself deep inside her, and tightly against her as her quivering began. I could swear that I heard a train whistle blowing as I watched her facial lips pucker into an "O". My grip tightened, my pulse roaring in my ears as I drove us both toward the edge.

Her head tilted back, a cry escaping her lips, lost beneath the reverberation of the bass drum thudding through the wall. She trembled, her body wrapping around me in waves.

I growled against her shoulder, my own control slipping. "Look at me," I rasped, "Show me that pretty face."

Natalia turned, her blue eyes locking onto mine just as the final wave crashed over me. The second her gaze met mine, my tension snapped. I swelled. She pulsed. I throbbed. She gasped. I clenched against her, feeling every pulse, every shudder, every ragged breath between us, while holding locks of her hair firmly with my fist.

Everything inside me unraveled, pouring into her · months of wanting, of needing, spilled inside her. Beat after beat I spilled inside of her, consumed by her. She quivered as she accepted all of me...until. We collapsed against each other, lost in the haze. Our minds blurred. Our bodies were spent. But we were lost in that fog together.

The trembling overtook us both, our bodies still entwined, breathless. Neither of us moved right away, lingering in the warmth, in the quiet hum of something sacred. I could feel the damp aftermath of our recklessness between us, a tangible reminder of all we had just surrendered to. Natalia must have felt the source, too, because a giggle escaped her lips, light, breathy, and intoxicating. Soon we were both laughing, the sound soft and private, a secret only we could share.

She shifted, turning to face me, her arms draping lazily around my neck as her lips found mine again, slower this time, unrushed, savoring. Radiant. That was the only word I could grasp to describe her in that moment. But even radiant felt insufficient, like trying to capture the sun in the palm of my hand. The real word for what she was probably existed somewhere else in the universe, still light-years away, waiting to be discovered.

~ ~

"What...the *fuck*...was that?" Erin's voice was thick with disbelief. Then, as if just realizing things herself, she let out a breathless laugh. "Do you have *any* idea how turned on I am right now?"

What had happened then hit me, I had slipped into some kind of trance while telling my story. I had not been aware of where I was, who I was talking to. I had not held back. Not even a little.

Erin shook her head, shifting in her seat. "I swear to God, I'm so hot right now, I'd fuck that skanky-ass bartender just to take the edge off. Jesus Christ, dude. You are in the wrong fucking profession." She huffed, "Hubby's in for a night, that's for sure."

I barked out a laugh, shaking my head with a mild apology before saying, "Yeah, well... that one's been in the spank bank for a while."

Erin exhaled sharply. "I should hope so. Holy crap."

Before the tension could coil any tighter, the waitress appeared, oblivious to the wildfire sitting at our table.

"Need anything else?" she asked.

I smirked, exhaling as I leaned back. "Just a check, please."

Erin leaned in, eyes burning with curiosity. "So, you guys hooked up. Did it work? Did she stay? Boyfriend and girlfriend? Move in together? Pop out a couple of kittens?"

I smirked, shaking my head.

When we stepped out of that closet, we were connected. Emotionally entangled. There was no way that we were about to sit back down at a table with switchblade-fingered Valerie and let her shred the moment to pieces. But she was still our ride home. Instead, we gravitated toward the abandoned piano against the entryway wall. I slid onto the bench; Natalia settled onto my lap. Our fingers intertwined and drifted over the keys, not playing, just touching, like they were still discovering each other the way we had minutes before. The afterglow wrapped around us, thick and golden.

We shared a couple questions with one another. I remember she answered in whispers, her voice laced with quiet amusement. I was fascinated by her.

Then, just as effortlessly as she always did, Valerie crashed through the moment. Storming into the entryway, purse in hand, eyes blazing. Something had gone down with the gross guitar guy. She was done. "Let's go, fuckers," she snapped.

Natalia and I exchanged a glance, fingers still laced together as we stood. Neither of us spoke. We simply followed.

The drive home was quiet. Silence had hitched a ride with us, stretching himself out between the hum of the tires and the glow of the dashboard. But in that stillness, something felt right. Like the universe had shifted, again, aligning my orbit with Natalia's. And my body, my virility, thrived on the secret we carried. That a part of me was still inside of Natalia. That she would fall asleep tonight with me woven into her. Valerie had no idea. No one did. This was not just physical. This was not just sex. This was celestial.

From the back seat, I watched the soft glow of passing streetlights reflect off Natalia's face. Every shadow, every highlight traced the contours of something precious. And right there, in that moment, I knew. I loved her.

I wanted her to stay. More than anything, I wanted to take her home that night, to fall asleep with her in my arms instead of knowing she'd be somewhere else. But I also understood, we had been through something. A shift, a realignment. We needed time. She would need time. Time required to process where we stood with one another. Still, I hoped that what had happened between us had elicited enough energy for her to contemplate staying. Because the possibilities between us? They were endless.

~ ~

The next day passed in a blur, like a song I couldn't quite remember. By the second morning, I found myself on my old bike, pedaling hard, the wind stinging my face as I made my way to Valerie's house. I needed to see Natalia. When Valerie opened the door, her expression was neutral and distant. She shrugged nonchalantly. "She's gone."

I felt the words hit me like a punch. "Gone where?"

Her eyes softened, a flicker of something rare, sympathy, crossing her face before she spoke. "Warsaw."

"WHAT?!" Erin's voice broke the stillness like glass shattering.

The statement hung in the air like a dense, suffocating fog, wrapping around Erin, heavy and inescapable. The moment seemed to stretch, sluggish and warm, as though time itself had paused just to let Erin feel the weight of the story.

Her eyes began to shimmer, her voice barely a whisper as she asked, "WHY?"

I didn't have an answer. My lips pressed together, and I shook my head slowly, the gesture almost mechanical, as if trying to signal that I, too, was as lost as she was.

Erin's frustration boiled over. "Did you send her a message? A text? A letter? A fucking transatlantic carrier pigeon?" She laughed bitterly through the tears, wiping her face with a cocktail napkin.

I couldn't do anything but shake my head again, the answer was still the same, "No."

Erin let out a slow, defeated breath, inhaling as though bracing herself for a truth that would never come. Then she sighed, the weight of the unknown settling around us like an uninvited guest. "So, does the love for her just end there?"

I reached for Erin's hand, my fingers curling tightly around hers, offering what little comfort I could. The answer was quiet, but it was mine, and I meant it. My voice was steady, as I whispered a confident, "No".

Not every story fits between these covers.
Morgan saves the most personal ones for those who subscribe at
www.*TheKnightOfRomance*.com

An Invitation From Morgan Knight

My dear reader. I am so happy and grateful that you have sipped a sample of what my library has to offer. The stories of longing, passion, and desire never grow old to me. Though we've shared in this intoxicating flight of tales, I have one secret to spill.

The shelves do not end here.

There are more tales.

More chronicles that I've never dared to share.

And, more moments waiting to unfold in ink and flame.

If you have felt the slightest flicker of connection between these pages, then I would be honored to write to you directly. Visit www.*TheKnightOfRomance*.com There you will find a private door. Leave your name, and I will send you updates on stories only for those who wish to go deeper.

Our correspondence will be selective, refined, and entirely respectful of your time. Rest assured, your inbox will remain graciously undisturbed as you will only hear from me when I truly have something worth sharing.

Until we meet again.

Morgan Knight, The Knight of Romance

About The Author

Lane Roberts is a storyteller of sensual depth and emotional richness, crafting tales where desire burns and the heart yearns. With a background in comedy and psychology, he develops fiction driven characters with a passion to explore the secret corners of longing.

Lane blends each story together in *The Knight Of Romance* with a healthy heaping of heat, drizzled in heart, and dusted with humanity.

But Lane does not work alone.

Introducing Morgan Knight, a sophisticated curator of passion, a literary host who guides readers through his private library of sultry tales. Though fictional, Morgan is very real in spirit. He is eloquent, intimate, and always inviting you to explore what lies beneath the surface.

Together, Lane and Morgan prepare stories for the modern romantic. Those who believe that love can be both tender and thrilling, or elegant and raw.

To read more, perhaps even receive a private letter, or just unlock secret stories, visit www.*TheKnightOfRomance*.com

9 781967 851003